CHRISTINA DIAZ GONZALEZ

MOVING TARGET

SCHOLASTIC INC.

FOR MY SISTER, HOPE

Copyright © 2015 by Christina Diaz Gonzalez

This book was originally published in hardcover by Scholastic Press in 2015.

All rights reserved. Published by Scholastic Inc., *Publishers since 1920*. SCHOLASTIC and associated logos are trademarks and/or registered trademarks of Scholastic Inc.

The publisher does not have any control over and does not assume any responsibility for author or third-party websites or their content.

No part of this publication may be reproduced, stored in a retrieval system, or transmitted in any form or by any means, electronic, mechanical, photocopying, recording, or otherwise, without written permission of the publisher. For information regarding permission, write to Scholastic Inc., Attention: Permissions Department, 557 Broadway, New York, NY 10012.

This book is a work of fiction. Names, characters, places, and incidents are either the product of the author's imagination or are used fictitiously, and any resemblance to actual persons, living or dead, business establishments, events, or locales is entirely coincidental.

ISBN 978-0-545-77319-5

10 9 8 7 6 5 4 3 2   17 18 19 20

Printed in the U.S.A.   40
First printing 2016

Book design by Phil Falco

—ONE—

There should have been some sort of warning. An ominous bird screeching across the sky or a strange animal howling in the distance. At the very least, it should have been a gloomy day. Better yet, it could have begun on an eerie night, under a full moon, near St. Peter's Square.

But it didn't.

It started on a typical blue-sky day in Rome, a day that looked like it had been peeled from the folds of one of the brochures for my school. It was that time of year when there was still a crispness in the air, but the days themselves were growing warmer with the promise of summer.

I unzipped my leather jacket and leaned against the bottom of the Bernini-like fountain that welcomed visitors to our campus. Daily living had washed away most of the novelty of having moved to Rome, though there was still something about the contrast of bright, pastel-hued Vespas zipping past the Colosseum that captured my imagination. Perhaps it was the fact that old and modern could blend together so effortlessly here, a feeling that this place transcended time. *"Everything is part of the same painting,"* as my dad liked to say. *"But we are each the artist of our own life. We choose what colors to use."*

I yawned, bored with my own thoughts. The problem was that in my life's painting there were only different tones of gray. It didn't matter what college town my dad moved us to, it all felt the same. Always the same classes, the same rules.

But this was Rome, the Eternal City. This wasn't Madison or St. Louis or Tallahassee. I had no excuse. No girl should be bored in this place.

I glanced over at the massive main gate. It remained closed to traffic, but a door next to it was unlocked so that the high schoolers could go out for lunch.

Maybe I could just walk out. Pretend to be a freshman. Who'd know? I'd been here less than a year and the words *eighth grader* were only stamped on my student ID, not my face. I could add some color to my life. Be more adventurous and explore the city a little bit.

Just do it, Cassie, I said to myself.

A bubbling sense of excitement filled me. I grabbed my small yellow messenger bag and slipped the strap across my body.

Casually, I strolled along the perimeter of the campus, making my way to the front gate. The smell of car exhaust from the Rome traffic drifted up the driveway toward me. I could see Via Tarsia through the fence's wrought-iron bars and imagined myself blending in with the other pedestrians, bicyclists, and motorists heading back to work—or, in my case, play. I'd get to see the real Rome, not the supervised one my father insisted on showing me. I would head out and go . . .

I stopped dead in my tracks.

Where *would* I go? I had no real plan. I could get in big

trouble and for what? I'd probably just waste my time drinking sodas at the small *osteria* down the street until it was time for my dad to pick me up from school. No, this was a stupid idea. I turned back around to face the school.

"Going somewhere, Miss Arroyo?" It was Professor Latchke, the most dreaded teacher in school.

"Um, no. Just getting some fresh air," I said, giving him my most innocent smile—the one where my brown eyes looked like they belonged to a cute little puppy. It always worked on my dad.

"Hmpf." His demeanor didn't change as he checked his watch. "You know, you really should consider spending a little more time studying for my class and a little less time daydreaming about leaving school."

"No, I mean, I wasn't daydreaming. It's lunchtime and I was just walking." What did this bald-headed, bow-tie-wearing, tweed-jacket-loving teacher have against me? I might not be a great student in his World History class, but I got good grades in my other classes. "It's not against the rules to wander around, is it?" My eyes met his.

"Of course not, Miss Arroyo. But like I've discussed with your father, you're not meeting your potential. You need to work harder."

A sinking feeling washed over me. He had called my dad? Because of a stupid C minus in his class?

"Today is a perfect example." He shook his head. "There was a review session for the upcoming test and instead of attending, you decided to spend your time staring at the gates. I believe your father has higher expectations of you. I'm sure he won't be pleased."

I bit my tongue. He was so wrong. My dad wasn't like that. We were a team. Papi always stressed that he had my back on everything. Even against mean, nasty teachers. He'd understand once I explained what was really going on.

"Time for you to take some responsibility for your academic career."

I shuffled my feet. "Uh-huh."

"That's 'yes, sir,' Miss Arroyo."

I looked down at the ground and mumbled, "Yes, sir."

He stood there for another few seconds, then slowly walked away.

I wanted to scream. Without a doubt, he was the worst thing about living in Rome.

I trudged over to a statue of Charlemagne riding into battle and plopped myself next to it. The shadow of the horse as it reared up on its hind legs cast an unusual image on the grass. It looked like a monster's mouth, gaping open with two large teeth about to chomp down. I imagined Professor Latchke being the monster's lunch. It made me feel a little better.

"Not eating today, Miss Arroyo?" The accent, the low-pitched voice, and the disappointment etched behind every syllable of my name sent a new wave of venom coursing through my veins.

No way. Was Professor Latchke going to torment me all day? Now he wanted me to eat lunch?

I slowly turned around. "Yes, sir. I already—" I stopped when I saw Simone holding back a smile. Her blonde, almost invisible eyebrows twitched with amusement. "Simone!" I exclaimed, throwing out a kick, which purposely missed the mark. "I hate when you do that!"

Simone let out a giggly, contagious laugh. "You love it when I prank *other* people." She paused and cleared her throat. "Isn't that ta-rue, Cah-sahn-drah?" This time she sounded exactly like our headmistress, Ms. Flemming.

I shook my head. "You, my friend, are an official freak of nature."

"Well, this freak is now completely done with her make-up quizzes." Simone did a little happy dance—one that was completely uncoordinated and made her tall, slender frame look like it was having convulsions. "Only bad thing is that it took up most of the lunch break."

"Serves you right for being sick all last week and leaving me here to fend for myself with all these *annoying americani*," I said in my best impression of an Italian, pointing to all the other American expat students scattered around in little clusters.

Simone grimaced. "That doesn't even sound close to an Italian accent."

"We can't all—"

"Hold on," she interrupted. "Here it comes. Just to make sure I don't have time to eat." She lifted her finger to the sky. "Wait for it. In three . . . two . . ."

The clanging sound drowned out her last word, and

students responded to the bell by moving across the large lawn like cattle going to the slaughterhouse. Except this slaughterhouse was disguised as an old Tuscan villa.

"Do we really have to go?" I tilted my head back, enjoying the feeling of my hair draping down my spine. "Latchke already hates me . . . I should at least do something to earn it."

"He doesn't hate you." Simone's eyes twinkled. "But what are you thinking?"

"I don't know." I gave her a sheepish grin. "Maybe tomorrow we make a run for it? Go explore Rome together?"

"Cassie Arroyo! Skipping class? That is not like you!" She put her fists on her hips, pretending to be shocked. She gave me a wink. "It sounds more like me. I must be rubbing off on you!"

I laughed. "Being me isn't exactly thrilling."

Simone let out a long, exaggerated sigh. "You've seen my life up close. Don't think you'd really want it." She gave me her hand. "C'mon, Miss Troublemaker. We'll be late to class if we don't hurry." She tried in vain to pull me up. "Really?" Simone let go of my arm. "You're just not going to go to class?" She took a step back. "What's with you?"

"Ugh." I rolled my eyes and stood. "I'm so tired of school. I can't wait for it to be over."

"Me too." She shrugged. "We'll do something fun this weekend—"

"CASSIE!" The frantic yell from across the field made Simone stop talking. There was no imitating that voice. I turned to see my father walking . . . no, running . . . no . . . *sprinting* toward us.

"It can't be," I muttered.

Simone turned to look, as did half the school.

"CASSIE!" he shouted again before stopping to put his hands on his knees and catch his breath. Apparently, the jog from wherever he had parked was as much exercise as any overweight forty-five-year-old art historian ever got. He stood again and motioned for me to come toward him.

"Latchke *called* him?" I shook my head in disbelief.

"Maybe it's something else," Simone said.

I sighed.

"NOW!" my dad commanded, unhappy with my delay.

"Never mind." Simone ran a finger across her throat. "You're dead."

I weaved around a few students and hurried over. "Papi, I can explain," I said. "Latchke's crazy intense, but I'm going to study for the test over the weekend."

I was prepared for almost any reaction—except for the one I got. My father lunged toward me and hugged me as tightly as he could. *"No importa,"* he muttered in Spanish. "I don't care."

"Papi?" I pulled away to look at him. He was wearing his normal work uniform—a dark-blue suit with a white shirt—but his hair was completely disheveled. It was rare to see him with even one hair out of place unless he was worried about something, and this was a whole head of worry. "What's wrong?" I asked.

"You know I love you, *m'ija*, right?" As he spoke, his eyes darted over to the Italian cypress trees that lined the school's boundary.

"I love you, too, but what's going on?"

"We have to go." He took my hand and started pulling me toward the main gate. "I'll explain in the car."

"Hold on." I quickened my step to keep up with him. "We're leaving? Don't you have to sign me out at the office?"

He didn't answer, just dragged me along as the last group of students rushed past us.

"Did something happen?" I asked, knowing he'd tell me the truth. After all, our policy was to never keep secrets. Even when I was young and he lost his job at the museum in Baltimore, he told me right away.

He put a hand on my back and ushered me past the tall gates and out to the street where our red Fiat was parked a few feet away. "Hurry up." He opened the car door and motioned for me to get in. "It's not safe here."

"Safe?" I tugged the seat belt across my shoulder as he rushed around the car and jumped into the driver's seat. "What do you mean? Should I get Simone?"

Before he could answer, a loud bang caused us both to duck for cover.

"STAY DOWN!" he ordered, peeling out and leaving a cloud of smoke behind us.

Doing exactly the opposite, I bolted upright and turned to see an old man, smothered in our car's exhaust smoke, standing on the sidewalk shouting obscenities at us in Italian.

"Papi, I think that was just a car backfiring some-where," I said, although my heart was beating so hard that it felt like it was going to pop right through my T-shirt and jacket.

"Maybe." He sped down the avenue, weaving between cars and zipping through two yellow lights.

I'd never seen him like this. He was usually so careful. Always driving five miles below the speed limit and complaining every time I begged him to let me drive for a little bit along the desolate country roads.

I grabbed the armrest as we made a sudden right turn instead of stopping at a light.

This was crazy.

At the next corner we made a last-minute left that sent me slamming against the door.

"SLOW DOWN!" I yelled, rubbing my upper arm. "You're going to get us killed!"

Papi glanced at the rearview mirror and took a deep breath. His shoulders dropped, and he eased off the gas. "Sorry," he mumbled and tried to turn the grimace on his face into a smile.

"What's going on?" I asked again. "We don't keep secrets from each other, remember?"

He stopped at the next red light and turned to face me, but didn't say anything. He just stared. Stared as if he could telepathically relay all sorts of information to me.

"Are you in some sort of trouble?"

"No, they won't hurt us if I—"

"Hurt us?" I interrupted. "Who would hurt us? What are you talking about?"

He took a deep breath and ran his fingers through his hair. "Don't worry . . . I'm going to fix things," he said in a voice barely above a whisper.

My stomach felt queasy. "Papi, I don't know what you've done, but you have to call the police . . . or the embassy." I pulled my cell phone out of my bag.

"No!" He snatched the phone and threw it on the floor.

I was shocked into silence.

"I'm sorry, Cassie," he said in a calmer voice. "We can't contact anyone. They have people everywhere." He shook his head. "I'd planned on talking to you about this since you were little." He paused for a moment. "It just never seemed like the right time. Gregorio was right."

"Since I was little? What are you saying? Who's Gregorio?"

"There's so much to tell you," he muttered.

He wasn't making any sense. "Papi, you're acting like you're about to say something crazy, like we're in the witness protection program or—" I paused. My by-the-book father was not a criminal, but he was certainly capable of having testified against one. "Is that it? Did you rat someone out? Is this something from when you lived in Cuba?"

BEEEEEP! BEEEEEP!

Startled, I glared at the man in the tiny two-seater car behind us. The light had just changed to green a fraction of a second earlier.

"HOLD ON!" I shouted back at him.

The response I got was another long BEEEEEEEP!

"Face forward and don't make eye contact, Cassie . . . with anyone." We were already crossing the intersection, blending in with the average insanity of Rome drivers. In the distance I could see the dome of the Vatican, but I had no idea where we were headed.

I gripped the sides of my seat as we swerved across several lanes and cut in front of a small delivery truck, making a sharp left onto Ponte Garibaldi to cross the Tiber River.

"Everything will be fine, Cassie." My dad kept his focus on the road, with only occasional glances in the rearview mirror. "Don't worry. I'm taking care of things. It's just very complicated."

"So un-complicate it!" I shouted, losing my patience.

"It's a long story." He shook his head and started to mumble to himself. "I just didn't think they'd trace the calls back to me. I thought I'd been careful. I only needed a little more time to find it . . ." He checked the rearview mirror again. "Okay, I guess it's time you knew. It starts with the Hastati." My father slowed the car and veered into a narrow cobblestoned alleyway that was lined with boarded-up apartment buildings.

"The what? You're not making sense."

"The Hastati. They're a secret organization." He abruptly stopped the car in front of a building tagged with graffiti and checkered with peeling posters for concerts that had come to Rome months earlier. "But I'll explain it all as soon as I'm done here. Just stay in the car."

"Stay here? What are we doing?"

"I'm getting us out of Italy. I just need to pick up some passports."

"We already have passports! Papi, this is crazy!"

"Listen." He grabbed me by the shoulders. "This is serious. I need you to stay down and out of sight until I get back." As my father slid out of the car, he lifted the back of his suit jacket and pulled out a gun.

"What the—?" I stared at the weapon as he placed it on the seat. "Have you gone completely insane?"

"You're safer in the car. Stay put and don't use the gun unless you absolutely have to. I'll be back in less than five minutes."

"No way!" I grabbed his sleeve before he could fully get out of the car. There was no chance I'd touch that gun, and since when did my dad even own one? "You tell me right now what's going on!"

My father scanned the empty alley. "Cassie, *m'ija*, we don't have time."

"I don't care. Either you tell me what you did or I'm . . . I'm . . ."

He pried my fingers off his sleeve. "I swear to you that I didn't do anything. Just lock the doors and stay out of sight."

My eyes jumped from him to the gun. Everything I knew about my father completely evaporated. "Someone's after you, and there has to be a reason for it. Tell me!"

"It's not me, Cass." He rubbed his face before giving me a look filled with dread. "It's you," he sighed. "Cassie, the Hastati are after you."

—TWO—

Crouched down, the gun beside me, my thoughts bounced from one idea to another. None of what my father said made any sense. Why would anyone be after me? And why was he getting us new passports? I had my brand-new Italy-stamped passport in my night table drawer at home.

I wiped my sweaty palms on the sides of my jeans and poked my head above the dashboard. The alley was desolate except for a stray cat, licking its paws, perched above a large dumpster. My eyes darted up the side of the building. Most of the windows were either shuttered or boarded up. Whoever lived here was not someone my dad normally hung out with.

I paused, an idea causing me to straighten up. My father had been working really long hours lately and barely sleeping. Even when I'd wake up in the middle of the night, he'd be at the kitchen table poring over books. Maybe exhaustion was making him have some sort of breakdown.

I fished my cell phone out from under the seat and texted Simone.

Dad freaking. Took me out of school. Get my stuff and I'll go by ur place later to tell u about it.

Not even two seconds later, I got a reply.

Where r u? All this bc of Latchke?

I smiled, thankful for some normalcy.

Somewhere in the Prati neighborhood I think. Not about Latchke. Not sure what it is.

A rattling noise made me look up just as I hit send. The alley cat had jumped off the dumpster and was scurrying toward a group of Vespas and motorcycles all parked together. *Enough is enough*, I thought. I needed some real answers.

I stuffed the phone in my pocket and threw open the door, but before I could get out, I spotted my dad dashing from the building.

Stepping out of the car, I took a defiant stance. He would either tell me what was going on or we weren't leaving.

"Get in!" he shouted as a motorcycle somewhere in the distance revved its engine.

"Wait." I put out my hand to stop him in midstride. "First, we need to—"

Before I could finish my sentence, a motorcycle zoomed by our car. The rider was dressed in black, with a black helmet that had red flames on the side. Dad hurtled toward me, knocking me to the ground. A popping noise filled the air.

"WHAT THE . . . ?" I pushed my father off me as he reached for the gun lying on the seat.

The sound of screeching tires filled the air. I twisted

around, and from underneath the car I could see white smoke as the motorcyclist did a one-eighty at the end of the alley and headed back toward us.

My dad staggered up. Took aim.

One . . . two . . . three shots.

I couldn't believe what I was seeing. My mild-mannered art historian father was in a gun battle. What kind of warped universe was I in?

The motorcyclist lost control and careened into the parked Vespas down the street, knocking them down like bowling pins.

"Go!" My dad pushed me into the car, ran to get in on the other side, and peeled out in reverse.

"That man! He was shooting at us!" I stared down the alley as the motorcyclist pushed a few bikes out of the way and started running after us.

"Just get down!" Our car swerved out of the alley as Papi shifted gears to get us moving forward.

I stayed silent and crouched down. Papi quickly turned onto several narrow streets, and then finally slowed down to blend with traffic along the main road.

I inched up in my seat and pulled out my cell phone. "I'm calling the police. We have to tell them that someone just tried to kill us."

"It's your phone!" Papi reached over, yanked the phone from my hand, and opened the car window. "That's how they found us."

It was clear what he was about to do. "DON'T!" I yelled, but it was too late. He flung the phone out into the street just in time for it to be run over by a tour bus.

"Why would you do that? How are we going to get help?" I was afraid my father was losing his mind. I wanted to yell some more, but then I saw it.

A bright-red blotch on his white shirt.

He looked down, too, and pressed his hand against the right side of his chest. The red stain got larger, blood seeping through his fingers.

"Papi, you've been shot!"

My father took a deep breath and focused on the road again. "Cassie, I always tried to protect you. You have to know that."

"Uh-huh." I ignored what he was saying. "We need to get you to a hospital."

He gave me a slight nod. "I know. There's one right over this bridge." He paused, his breathing becoming more labored. "You have to know that you can't trust anyone."

Up ahead I could see an ambulance pulling into a large brick building that looked like a fortress. "Okay, we'll tell the police and—"

"You can't trust them, either. We don't know who might be involved with the Hastati." He pulled up behind the ambulance. "As soon as I get inside, you need to run. Go find Brother Gregorio at the San Carlo Monastery. He can help."

"Run away?" I glanced over at my father; his normal olive complexion had turned ashen. "No way. I'm not leaving you."

"You have to." He shifted the car into park. "It's too dangerous for you to stay." He moaned while getting something from his jacket. "Take this with you," he said, pulling out a yellow envelope from his suit pocket. "Always remember that I love you . . . to the moon and back."

"Don't talk like that. Just give it to me later." I waved it off, but he placed the envelope on my lap anyway.

"Take it." He slumped against the door, eyes closed.

"Papi!" There was no time to waste. *"Aiuto! Aiuto!"* I yelled in Italian while jumping out of the car.

"No, no!" A paramedic jerked his hands around, motioning for us to move the car. *"Non si può parcheggiare qui!"*

I ignored him. There was no time to worry about proper parking when my dad was hurt—maybe dying. *"Mio padre . . . morendo,"* I shouted back at him with my mangled Italian as I ran around the car and opened the driver-side door. *"¡Está herido!"* I added in Spanish, because I'd forgotten the Italian word for injured and figured this might be close enough.

My father almost fell out of the car, but I propped him back up. "Cassie, Brother Gregorio . . . at the San Carlo Monastery," he whispered. "He's the only one who can help us." He glanced over at the yellow envelope resting against the gearshift. "Take that and go." His eyes grew glassy. "Promise me," he pleaded. *"Por favor, m'ija."*

"Brother Gregorio," I repeated, not wanting to forget. "Got it." I gave my dad's hand a gentle squeeze as the paramedic pushed me aside. "I'll go as soon as I know you're okay."

The moment the paramedic saw my father was bleeding from a gunshot wound, he began calling in Italian for other people to come. I only understood something about a weapon and the *polizia*.

With what seemed like his last ounce of strength, Dad shoved the paramedic away and pulled me closer. "Cassie, if you love me, please go. Now." The intensity of his voice was chilling. "Your life . . . and so much more . . . depends on it. Promise me, please."

Tears were welling up in my eyes. I couldn't believe this was happening.

His hand trembled as he touched my cheek. "Cass . . ." He could barely get my name out.

I nodded, not wanting him to waste any more energy. "Okay, I promise, Papi. I promise."

—THREE—

My fingers gripped the steering wheel. I had no idea where I was supposed to go. The nurses who had taken my father away had wanted me to follow them in, but I'd told them that I needed to wait for my mother outside. They seemed to buy the lie, giving me a few minutes to pull my thoughts together.

I really did wish I was waiting for my mother—or any relative—to show up. But there was no one else to depend on; it was just my dad and me. The way it had always been.

I glanced around. The hospital's emergency entrance was now eerily quiet after the frenzied activity only minutes earlier. Was I really supposed to just leave my dad here, even if that's what I promised him?

The yellow envelope my dad had given me lay next to the gearshift.

It was just one of those ordinary mustard-colored envelopes with the metal clasp on the flap, except this one had been folded in half and tied with a blue cord.

As I picked it up and slipped off the cord, I saw that my dad had left a smear of blood across it. Inside, I could see American passports and a couple of notebooks bound together by a rubber band. I stuck my hand in to pull the items out, but a loud knock at my window made me jump.

"*Signorina, va bene?*" a police officer asked me.

I quickly closed the envelope and put it under my legs. "Yes, I'm fine . . . *tutto bene*," I said through the raised window. "Just waiting for someone."

The police officer stared inside the car, checking things out. My heartbeat quickened as I realized that my father's gun was still under the seat. Could my dad—or even I—get arrested if it were found? I tried to stay calm, but tears started to form behind my eyes.

The officer finally pursed his lips and muttered something about no-parking zones before turning on his heel and walking away.

I let out a big sigh of relief, but it was obvious I couldn't stay here much longer without raising suspicion. But where should I go? I couldn't imagine going home by myself right now. Whoever shot my dad probably knew where we lived. And without my phone I had no idea how to find Brother Gregorio.

"Simone," I muttered to myself. At her place I'd be safe and could try to find out more about Brother Gregorio and the San Carlo Monastery. All I had to do was find a metro station, and then I'd be able to figure out how to get to her house.

Taking a deep breath, I tried to muster up every ounce of courage I had. "You can do this, Cassie," I told myself. "You can be brave."

I grabbed the envelope, stuffed it in my bag, and got out of the car. The moment I stepped outside, a wave of panic at being completely unprotected hit me. Immediately, I jumped back into the car.

I would move it away from the entrance and take a moment to calm myself. I started the car and let it roll out of the driveway. I was approaching the hospital exit when something in one of the side-view mirrors caught my eye.

A man in black clothes and a dark-tinted helmet with flames on the side had parked his motorcycle right in front of the hospital entrance, the same place I'd been a few moments earlier. My car was partially hidden by a delivery van, so I stayed put and watched as he took off his helmet, revealing curly dark hair and light skin. He placed his helmet on the motorcycle. There was no way I could be sure if this was the guy who had just shot my father, but it was too much of a coincidence. I couldn't take the chance and let him go inside and finish the job. I had to do something.

I pushed down on the car horn as hard as I could.

BEEEEEEEEEEEP!

I rolled down the window. "Hey!" I yelled and waved my arm. "Over here!"

The man paused, looked my way, then ran toward me.

I floored the gas pedal, hitting the curb of the driveway before peeling out toward the main avenue. In the rearview mirror I could see him turning back—probably to get his motorcycle, but it didn't matter because I was already turning the corner, darting in front of a bus, and merging into Rome's traffic.

My heart was beating faster than ever and my breath was coming in and out in short little puffs. Hopefully I'd managed to get him away from my father, but for how long?

Stopping at a red light, I checked the rearview mirror. There was no sign of the guy on the motorcycle. Maybe I was safe for now.

The light changed and I slowly moved the car forward. Cars were beeping at me as I tightly clenched the steering wheel. I pulled over onto a quiet street, knowing that I was only going to draw more attention to myself if I kept driving.

"Think, Cassie . . . THINK!" I said out loud.

Driving in Rome was incredibly confusing—it wasn't at all like the times Papi let me try driving on the empty country roads. In Rome, there were one-ways, dead ends, and streets that circled around to bring you back to where you started. I might drive myself right into the gunman's path. My only option was to find a metro station.

I grabbed my bag and ventured out, keeping my head down to avoid being recognized.

After what seemed like an hour of aimless roaming, I stumbled across the Valle Aurelia metro station. Running down the steps, I stopped to read the subway map and saw that I was on a direct line to Spagna—the station closest to Simone's place. My hand shook as I pulled out my metro card. From where I stood, I could hear the screeching sound of a train arriving. I pushed through the turnstile, my heart beating fast and hard as I ran to the train and jumped aboard.

There were only a few people in the subway car, but I couldn't take any chances. I grabbed a newspaper from the floor and hid behind it until I reached my destination.

Exiting the Spagna Station, I became almost giddy with the knowledge that I'd soon be safe. I ran down the block, sideswiping a woman wearing ridiculously high heels, before reaching the three-story building.

"Please let Simone be home," I prayed, checking over my shoulder and then pressing the doorbell.

"*Alo?*" the housekeeper answered through the speaker.

"Niurka, it's Cassie. Can you buzz me in?" I eyed two kids passing by on their skateboards.

"Who?"

"Niurka!" Simone called out from somewhere in the background. "Let her in!"

"Yes, of course, Miss Simone."

A long buzz and a click unlocked the front door.

"Miss Simone is upstairs," Niurka said, barely looking at me as she headed out and I rushed in. "Tell her I'll be back with the groceries in a little while."

Once inside, an overwhelming sense of relief washed over me.

"Get on up here!" Simone called out from the top of the circular stairs. "Are you in a ton of trouble? Did your dad completely flip about your grade?"

Simone's smile disappeared when she saw the expression on my face.

"What's wrong?" she asked, slowly coming down the stairs.

I tried to move and my knees began to buckle. It was as if all the adrenaline that had been coursing through my body had suddenly been sucked out, leaving me with nothing.

"Cassie." Simone took the remaining steps two at a time. "You're scaring me."

I crumpled to the ground. "Everything is so messed up. I don't know what to do."

"Did something happen with your dad? You two have a fight or something?" Simone crouched down next to me. "You know you can stay here. It's just me and Niurka most of the time anyway."

"That's not it." I took a deep, shaky breath. Then another.

Simone waited for me to explain, but I couldn't. I didn't know what was happening. I didn't even know if my father was okay. The only thing that was certain was that he was depending on me and I couldn't let him down.

I had to pull it together.

I *would* pull it together.

"Your computer," I muttered, standing up. "I need to use it."

"Um, okay." Simone nodded, confused at my sudden shift of moods. "Mind telling me what's going on?"

"Don't know if you'd even believe me."

"It can't be that bad. I've probably been in just as much trouble."

I gave her a halfhearted smile. "Then I guess it's just your average someone-wants-to-kill-me kind of day."

—FOUR—

It was a scene that had played out a hundred times since I'd moved to Italy: Simone on her bed checking her cell phone and me sprawled on the papasan chair her mother had shipped over from Indonesia. Only everything felt different now.

"I just can't believe you got shot at," Simone said, looking up the hospital's phone number while I searched on her laptop for information on Brother Gregorio and the San Carlo Monastery. "It's like a James Bond movie or something."

"Yeah, except my dad is *not* James Bond." I paused to read the link I'd found about the San Carlo Monastery. It had a small map, but didn't say much except that it was considered an inactive monastery. "Do you think inactive means abandoned?" I asked Simone.

"Who knows?" She pointed to the phone. "You still want me to call the hospital?"

I nodded. "Your Italian is better." I got off the chair, walked to the antique desk, and grabbed the screenshot I'd sent to print. "This place is a couple of blocks from the Colosseum. Do you think—"

"Shh." Simone held up a finger. In the nasal voice of Headmistress Flemming, she asked the other person on the line about the condition of Felipe Arroyo.

I folded the paper and put it in my messenger bag, which I'd kept slung across my body. Shifting my weight from foot to foot, I stood in front of Simone. A lump had formed in my throat. I needed to hear that my dad was okay, because if he wasn't . . .

I shook my head and pushed away the thought. He would be fine. He had to be.

After a brief pause, Simone whispered, "Sit." She tapped the bed. "They have me on hold."

I stayed standing and fidgeted with the bag's strap. I couldn't waste any more time. The moment Simone got information on my dad, I'd head out to find Brother Gregorio.

"Seriously. You might as well sit because you're not leaving without me anyway."

I scrunched my eyebrows. It was one thing to stick together and maybe skip school one day, but this was totally different. "I don't think that's a good idea."

Simone shrugged. "I'm not asking for permission."

"Um, didn't you hear me earlier? Someone wants to kill me. As in shoot me. With a real gun. And bullets."

"Uh-huh." She looked at me as if that were nothing. "So?"

"So?! You could get killed! I'm probably already putting you in danger by just being here." I paced back and forth in front of the bed.

"Look, calm down. You're the best friend I've ever had . . . strike that, closest thing to family I've ever had, so I *am* going." She cocked her head to the side. "Got it? And when I'm done here, we'll call a driver to take us wherever we want. I'll leave Niurka a note so she doesn't worry when she gets back from her errands."

I plopped down beside her, grateful for the help but feeling guilty about wanting it. "Okay." I gave her a little nudge. "Thanks." My mind went back to my father. "Aren't they taking a really long time? Maybe you should hang up and call again."

Simone shook her head and raised a finger. *"Che?"* Simone asked in her disguised voice. *"Mio nome?"* She bit her lip and looked at me. I shrugged.

"Signora Flemming," Simone continued with a smile.

Immediately, I shook my head and mouthed, "Nooo!"

But it was too late. Simone was on a roll.

"Della accademia," she finished saying. Another pause. *"Grazie."*

She covered the phone with her hand. "What?"

"You should've used a fake name."

Simone pursed her lips together before lifting the phone back to her ear. "Well, I didn't say what school I was from. Plus, it's too late now."

"I guess."

The hospital seemed to take forever to get back to Simone. I hoped it wasn't because there was bad news. I paced around the room a few times and peered out the second-floor window to check for the motorcyclist. The only odd person out there was a man in a dark suit sitting on a bench across the street. He looked out of place, although I couldn't figure out why.

I picked up Simone's camera and zoomed in on the guy's face. A crooked nose and hardened stare gave him the look of a boxer. But what set him apart was the fact that he was missing a large part of his left ear. He turned his head just as I snapped a photo, but I was able to get enough to show Simone.

"You ever see this guy before?" I asked.

"No, but don't worry," Simone said, trying to relieve the concern that was obviously written across my face. "We're perfectly safe in here. My mother bought this place from an ambassador or some sort of diplomat. It's built like a fortress. Anyway, the guy is probably just waiting for a ride or something."

"Yeah, I guess."

"Trust me, my mother is a freak about security. We're fine here."

"I'm going to have to meet your mom one of these days." As soon as I said the words, I wanted to kick myself. I knew better than to bring up her mother.

"Yeah, if she ever spends more than five hours in the same city as me."

As much as Simone pretended to sympathize with all my complaining about my dad's overprotective, hawklike treatment, I knew she secretly craved some of it.

Thinking of my father, I opened my bag and took out the yellow envelope, my fingers lingering on the smeared blood. I pulled out the two passports and flipped the first one open.

There I saw my picture, but not my name. Instead, it said I was Mia Sanchez. The other had my father's picture with the fake name of Alberto Sanchez.

I put both passports in my messenger bag, and then took out the two books that were still in the envelope. The first one was dark blue with gold etching and looked relatively new, while the other one had a worn leather-bound cover. I put the blue notebook inside my bag to read later and focused on the old one. The handwriting inside was unfamiliar and difficult to read, and the words seemed to be Latin, but, on the second page, one word leapt out at me:

Hastati.

The secret group my dad had said wanted me dead.

I tried to understand the sentence, but besides me not being able to read Latin, most of it was smudged and illegible. I walked over to the window and held the notebook at an angle, trying to see the words in a better light. The sun hovered just above the roofline of the building across the street.

I glanced out the window one more time and noticed the half-eared guy was gone. I'd been worried for nothing. I flipped through the notebook again and paused on a random page where one sentence seemed to be written in dozens of languages. I could read the ones in English, Spanish, and Italian, and they all said the same thing.

The Guardian will be bound for life once the spearhead is used.

"No, no, signora." Simone raised her voice. *"Per favore."*

I looked back at Simone.

"Guardare di nuovo," Simone pleaded. *"Felipe Arroyo."* She repeated the name, spelling it out for them.

Something was wrong. Very wrong.

I put the notebook down on the bed and got closer to Simone.

"Un momento." Simone covered the phone with her hand and whispered, "Does he go by any other name?"

"No." I swallowed the lump forming in the back of my throat. The sunshine coming in through the window, which had felt warm and inviting, was now hot and suffocating. "Why?"

"The stupid receptionist is saying that she doesn't find that name in her system."

Could my dad have used the name that was on the fake passport? "Have her try the name Alberto Sanchez."

Simone nodded, returning to the phone conversation. *"Forse il—"*

A loud pop behind me drowned out her last words. I spun around to see the window splinter. Cracks ran across it like the threads of a spiderweb, but it held together. Within a second, something else hit the glass.

"Get down!" I yelled, pushing Simone to the floor.

Simone cursed at the top of her lungs.

I scrambled out of the bedroom as the bulletproof glass was pelted with more shots. Simone ran past me and dove under a small wooden coffee table in the middle of the upstairs sitting room.

"That's not going to help!" I yelled.

She crawled back out and flashed me a key that had been taped to the underside of the table. "I know! We need to go!" she exclaimed.

My thoughts flashed to the movies I'd seen where the super rich had places they could hide in case of an attack. "A safe room?"

"Better," she answered, racing down the hallway. "A way out!"

She opened a closet and tossed aside a couple of fur coats, revealing a small door. Unlocking it with the key, she pushed it open. "C'mon . . . hurry!" she called, hunching down and carefully stepping through to the other side.

I followed, closing both the closet and the secret door behind me. Immediately, I was engulfed in darkness, with the only light coming from Simone's cell phone a few feet below. The secret door led to a narrow shaft with metal rungs leading all the way down.

After climbing down at least ten feet, I still couldn't see the bottom. "Where does this thing go?" I whispered, afraid that someone entering the apartment might hear us.

"Erghf bulaks," Simone incoherently answered, the cell phone in her mouth lighting the area below as she held on to the side rails and lowered herself onto the next rung.

After fifty or sixty feet, we finally hit dank, but solid,

ground. Simone, her phone in her hand again, swung it from side to side, lighting up the area. Rats and roaches skittered by our feet.

"Ughhhh!" Simone hopped from leg to leg to avoid them as they took refuge from the light.

We were in a dirty cavern and, besides the shaft above us, the only way out seemed to be a wide tunnel with a cobblestoned floor that stretched into more darkness.

"The notebook!" I shouted with the sudden realization of what I'd done. I could picture the old leather journal sitting on Simone's bed. "I left it in your room! We have to get it!" I put my hand back on one of the metal rungs and started climbing up.

"Are you crazy?" Simone pulled me down by my pants. "You can't go there now."

"But I think it was important. My father gave it to me and . . . and—" I felt like I was going to be sick.

"And nothing. We have to keep moving."

I knew she was right, but I couldn't leave one of the biggest clues to whatever was happening just lying on Simone's bed.

"Listen, once we get to Brother Gregorio's we'll find a way to get it back. When the coast is clear," Simone suggested. "Okay?"

I nodded and touched my bag, making sure that the other notebook was still in there.

"I'm really sorry about all of this, Simone. I don't even know how they found me." I paused, fighting tears of guilt and helplessness. "You should probably get far away from me."

"No way." Simone aimed the phone's flashlight into the blackness. "Plus, who's to say these people won't come after me anyway? If they're at my house, then they already know I'm involved. We're sticking together until we figure some things out." She pointed to the tunnel. "We need to go."

She grabbed my hand and we ran side by side, the bottom of my jeans getting splashed with the putrid water that puddled in between the gaps of the cobblestones. It felt like we'd run at least half a mile when Simone abruptly stopped.

I jumped as a couple of squeaking rats ran in between my legs. "What?"

Simone shined the light on the stone wall up ahead. We'd reached the end.

"We're here," she said.

"But it's a dead end." I walked forward and knocked on the solid rock, my pulse quickening. "And I didn't see any doors along the way."

Simone came and stood right next to me. A high-pitched screech filled the tunnel as she pushed on a few of the concrete blocks that lined the sides.

A grin that would make the Cheshire cat jealous spread across her face. "Who said anything about a door you can see?"

—FIVE—

There were about ten large cement blocks held in place by a hinge, so when Simone pushed hard enough, they swiveled inward to reveal a small room. Actually, it was more of a closet, with a dusty mop and empty bucket in one corner and gray metal flooring that had begun to rust.

As we stepped inside, the ground beneath us began to tremble and shake. "Where are we?" I asked.

Simone fumbled with the key she'd taken from her house and tried to open the door that was on the other side of the room. "Spanish Steps . . . well, somewhere under the Spanish Steps. In the metro tunnel." She pulled open the door as a subway car rushed past, the wind knocking her back into me.

Cautiously, Simone stepped onto a narrow ledge that ran along the tracks. I followed her out, hugging the wall in case another train approached.

"So which way do you think we should go?" Simone asked as I closed the door behind me. It was plastered with fake warnings that there was no entry due to high voltage.

"Me? How would I know? I thought this was your escape plan." I glanced up and down the tunnel.

"Um, hello? I was nine when my mother bought the place. She forced me down here with the rats and roaches, because she said if I chose to live in Rome I needed to know

34

how to save myself." Simone shook her head. "Who does that to a kid? Made me think twice about leaving Praiano."

"Sorry." It was all I could think to say. "I'm glad you came here, though."

Simone sighed. "Yeah, me too. Wouldn't have had the chance to become friends with you if I kept living in that little town."

"Um, considering what's going on with me now," I said with a smile, "you might want to rethink that."

"Hm." Simone held out her hands as if weighing her options. "Hanging out with a bunch of servants, in a fortress of a house, without ever having the chance to make any real friends versus living in a big city full of people, fashion, and excitement." She gave me a nudge. "Yeah, not a tough choice."

"I guess." It was the most Simone had ever talked to me about her life before moving to Rome.

I noticed that the tunnel had now grown quiet and stopped vibrating, but it was only a matter of time before another train passed dangerously close to us. "Let's go that way." I pointed to the left. "I think the train we saw was picking up speed, so the platform is probably in that direction. Worst case we'll double back if I'm wrong."

"Worst case we get hit by a train," Simone said with a smirk.

We inched along the ledge, around a big curve, and in less than a minute the platform widened and we saw several people standing on the Spagna Station platform, waiting for the next train. At first I was worried that someone would question two girls popping out of the tunnel, but the waiting crowd was either oblivious or too jaded to care.

Without saying another word, Simone and I mixed in with a group of women standing under a sign showing that there were two minutes until the next train. We scooted back, closer to the wall, keeping an eye on everyone around us. I couldn't help thinking about my father's warning: Anyone could be a threat.

From behind me, a tanned, wrinkled hand touched my shoulder, causing me to jump.

"Just a coin or two," said an old, haggard woman, stretching open her palm while leaning against a mangled cane. "For my family," she added in heavily accented English.

I thought of *my* family . . . my dad. Was he alive? Was he in pain?

"Vattene!" Simone shooed the old woman away before I could even say anything.

The old woman sneered. "Remember, the choices we make determine our destiny," she said ominously before turning toward another couple on the platform.

Simone ignored her and took a couple of steps forward. The crowd had started to move closer to the yellow safety line painted on the floor as the light from an approaching train lit up the underground station.

My eyes stayed on the old woman. There were homeless people and gypsies everywhere in Rome, but something was different about this woman and it wasn't only the fact that she spoke to me in English. She slowly turned back around and our eyes locked. Neither of us blinked, each studying the other, until the corners of her lips began to curl up and she gave me a smile that showed her rotting teeth.

The rumbling of the subway cars and howling of the brakes filled the station.

"Cassie!" Simone called out to me as the crowd pressed her forward.

"The choices we make determine our destiny!" the old woman shouted.

I stood transfixed. Behind me the doors of the subway cars exhaled as they opened to allow throngs of passengers in and out.

"Cassie!" Simone grabbed my hand. "We've got to go." She pulled me away and we quickly maneuvered our way around several people until we boarded the second subway car.

"Colosseum, that's where you said we had to go, right?" Simone asked, grabbing hold of the car's center pole.

"Mm-hm." I took the window seat next to her and pulled out the map I'd printed at Simone's apartment. "This was the only Monasterio San Carlo I could find." I looked at the subway map plastered above the doors and compared it with the map I held in my hand. "I think we get off at Vittorio Emanuele Station without changing trains."

Simone took a deep breath. "Good," she muttered.

I leaned my head against the window. It was strange, but I felt safer in the crowd because we looked like just two average girls on a subway. Now that I was able to settle down, my thoughts drifted to what I'd say to Brother Gregorio. I had so many questions, but they all boiled down to two things: Where was my dad? And why were people after me?

The train lurched forward and slowly pulled away from the station. I looked out at the terminal. People had filtered down the stairs, filling the void we'd left. It was business as usual, nothing but a typical Thursday afternoon in Rome. At least for most people.

In the corner of the subway platform, I spotted the old woman asking a businessman for money. Her words still rang in my head.

Choices determine destiny.

It was similar to something my dad used to tell me when I was little. He'd remind me of how my mother would always say that the beauty of life was its uncertainty. How you could choose your own future and nothing was preordained.

It had never been more true.

I had to choose to be brave.

—SIX—

The feeling of being someone's prey was beginning to take its toll. I evaluated everyone around me. The couple holding hands boarding the subway car, the police officer crossing the street right by the station's exit, the tour group being led by a woman wearing a big hat, even the old man feeding the pigeons . . . they were all potential assassins.

"This way." Simone pointed to her right without looking up from the GPS map on her phone.

We rounded the corner, stepping into the shadows of the buildings around us. The sun was so low that the only rays of sunlight were at the intersections.

"I really don't think you should keep using your phone," I said, thinking back to how mine had been thrown out of the car. "They might be able to track us."

Simone ignored me and crossed the street, her blonde hair flashing as she stepped in—and then out—of the sunlight. "They don't know my number and we don't even know who *they* are." She glanced down at her phone one more time. "Plus, I had to try to reach my mom . . . not that she ever picks up for me. But it doesn't matter," she said, shutting off the phone. "We're here."

I stared at the nondescript building with the green door. The windows had lattice-style ironwork covering the openings, and they seemed to be boarded up from the inside.

Other than a relief above the door that showed an ornate cross being held on either side by an angel, nothing about the building looked particularly religious. But the bronze plaque above the doorbell had the number twenty-four on it. This had to be the place.

"Someone better be home," I muttered, pressing the buzzer while keeping an eye on the desolate street.

Nothing.

I knocked on the door and held the buzzer down for a full three seconds. "Hello?" I shouted. "Anyone there?"

"Maybe we should keep moving," Simone suggested, her back up against the building's wall.

"No. Brother Gregorio's here." I paused, knowing that there was no plan B. "He has to be."

I pounded the door with the side of my fist until it hurt. Just as I was about to start with a barrage of kicks, there was a clank on the other side. Simone and I stood still. We could hear two more locks being undone, followed by the screeching sound of metal being dragged.

The door creaked open a few inches, but I could only see part of a person's face.

"Brother Gregorio?" I asked.

"No." The door opened a little wider to reveal a guy, a little older than us, with light-brown hair, tan skin, and greenish-gray eyes that looked almost transparent. "I'm Asher," he said in perfect English. "Come in. Brother Gregorio has been expecting you."

"He has?" I asked as the door opened wide and I stepped forward. Standing next to him, I noticed that he was six or seven inches taller than me. He was wearing loose-fitting jeans, a gray polo, and a hoodie. He didn't match what I imagined a monk or a monk-in-training would look like.

Simone tried to follow me in, but Asher raised his left hand and stopped her. "I'm sorry, only she comes in," he said. I noticed the large silver ring he was wearing.

"She's with me," I explained.

He raised a single eyebrow. "Brother Gregorio didn't mention another girl."

"Really?" Simone cocked her head to the side. "Maybe Brother Gregorio doesn't tell you everything."

His eyes narrowed as he stared at Simone. "I'll check with him, but you'll have to wait out here for now."

"Listen, Asher—that's your name, right?" He nodded as I stepped outside and stood next to Simone. "We're in trouble, but either both of us come in or neither of us do."

Asher's eyes darted back and forth between us.

"Who is she and why is she here?" he asked.

I hesitated. What was I supposed to say? That she was my best friend, and some unknown bad guys were chasing us around Rome trying to kill us, and that my father had sent me here to see a monk I'd never met before? It sounded insane.

"*That* is none of your business. Brother Gregorio is expecting us." Simone pushed Asher aside, and with me at her heels, we both moved past the doorway. "Now, are you going to do your job and go get him?" she asked, her arms crossed and impatience in her voice. I'd never heard Simone speak like that. It didn't even sound like her.

I could see Asher's jaw tense, but he reached behind us to close the door, locking it with three dead bolts. "Stay here," he commanded before rushing up some nearby stairs, taking them three steps at a time.

Simone and I exchanged a look. Immediately, we started wandering around, checking out the place. We were in a covered breezeway that surrounded a small courtyard. The garden was full of all types of potted plants, some the size of small trees, and in the center there was a large fountain, which was covered in a mosaic of broken tiles. A large skylight above the courtyard revealed clouds tinged with hints of pink and purple.

"Pretty good impression, right?" Simone said in a hushed voice.

"Huh?"

"The way I handled that guy. Totally my mom." She crouched down to smell a yellow rose. "I was impersonating my mother. You got that, right?"

"Well, I knew something was up," I said, slowly walking around the fountain. Even though we'd reached our destination, I felt like a deer on high alert; all my senses were twitching, searching for anything that might be out of place.

All around the courtyard were French doors that revealed different rooms. I peeked in as I passed, catching glimpses of a kitchen, dining room, and living room. A few other doors had lace curtains for privacy.

"I told you both to stay put!" I looked up. Asher was leaning over the railing right above us.

"We know what you said," Simone answered coolly, tracing her hand along the edge of the fountain. "Just go find Brother Gregorio."

"Please," I added, trying to soften things up.

"That's what I'm doing." He glared at Simone. "And I'm very glad *you* are not Cassandra."

—SEVEN—

"He even knows my name," I muttered the moment Asher disappeared into one of the rooms.

"Yeah." Simone scowled. "And I don't like his attitude." She paced around the courtyard. "My gut says that guy is bad news."

"Actually, Asher's quite the opposite." The voice came from an older man who had stepped out of an elevator at the far end of the courtyard. Unlike Asher, he looked exactly how I expected a monk to look. He had a wiry gray beard and wore a brown friar's robe with a small rope tied around his very large waist. He walked slowly, but his eyes never left mine. He paused briefly beneath one of the breezeway arches.

"Brother Gregorio?" I asked, my voice hesitating. I had expected him to speak to me in Italian, not in English.

"None other." He smiled warmly. "And you are the lovely Cassandra. At long last we meet." His eyes shifted to Simone as we both walked toward him. "You are a friend of Cassandra's, I gather?"

"Um, yes, sir." Simone did a half-bow, half-nod thing in acknowledgment.

"Very well." Brother Gregorio scanned the courtyard, then looked back at me. "And Felipe . . . where is he?"

At the mention of my father, my lower lip quivered.

Brother Gregorio tensed up and his face hardened into a grimace. "I see. Something has happened . . . as I feared."

Tears stung my eyes. "He was shot, and the hospital I took him to says that he's not there." My voice was getting squeaky. I took a deep breath, keeping my emotions in check. "He told me to find you. That you'd help."

"There, there." He tapped my shoulder. "Felipe is a strong, stubborn man. He'll be fine, and you're safe here until we can sort things out." He pointed down the breezeway. "Come. We'll speak in my office." Wobbling from side to side with each step, he led us to a door with a small gold cross hanging on the front. He reached for the doorknob, but stopped before turning it.

"I'm sorry, child." Brother Gregorio put a wrinkled hand on Simone's arm. "This is a conversation for me and Cassandra to have in private."

"No," I countered. "We went through this earlier when that guy Asher didn't want to let her in. Simone stays with me."

Brother Gregorio shook his head. "Cassandra, that is not the way these things work. She cannot be privy to what we are going to discuss."

"Don't worry, Cassie." Simone took a couple of steps back. "I can wait out here."

"Yes, that would be best." Brother Gregorio gave Simone a gentle smile. "I can see you are a good friend."

I faced Simone. "No, I want you to hear what is going on." There was too much at stake for me to face everything alone. Even with Simone by my side I wasn't sure if I could deal with whatever came next. "I need you with me. Plus, I got you into this mess. The least I can do is have you be there when I find out what this is all about."

"Un momento." Brother Gregorio paused. "Please tell me you have some understanding of what is going on, Cassandra."

I stayed silent.

His eyes felt like they were penetrating my thoughts, searching for something and not finding it. "Holy smoke!" He threw his hands up in the air. "Didn't Felipe tell you anything?"

"Well, he said to find you." I bit my lip. This wasn't the answer he wanted to hear. "We didn't have much time and—"

"Time?" Brother Gregorio shook his head in disgust. "I've warned him. Told him this might happen. Now look at us." He turned to face the door, pulling out a key from under his cloak. "I must insist that your friend stay out here."

I hesitated. If the only way to get answers and help my father was to leave Simone outside, then I had no choice. I had to do it.

"Go," Simone whispered in my ear. "I'll be right here and you can fill me in later. Just don't trust him too much."

I followed the old monk into a small room with a round stained-glass window that scattered the dying sunlight into a prism of colors over the floor. Dust particles hovered in space over the stacks of books that filled the room. But more than books, there were papers, some yellowed with age, everywhere. There were piles, teetering on the edge of toppling over, on the floor, hanging off bookshelves, and covering the large desk that was pushed to the corner of the room.

"Have a seat." Brother Gregorio pointed to a high-backed red velvet chair. The seat held a mound of papers on it, which left no place to sit.

"Oh, right." Brother Gregorio noticed the mess around him. "It looks disorganized, but I know where everything is. You can put those papers on the floor next to you." He plopped himself down on a tattered and torn brown leather chair. "So"—he drew in a deep breath and slowly let it out— "tell me what happened today and what you know."

I placed the stack of papers on top of some others under my chair and sat down. "My father picked me up from school early and was freaked out about something. He mentioned the Hastati, but I'm not sure what or who that is. He said you could help me."

"Mm-hm." Brother Gregorio pressed his fingertips together as if praying and tapped his lips. "Go on."

When I explained how we'd been shot at by the guy on the motorcycle, Brother Gregorio barely reacted, only stopping to jot down some notes, even when I told him someone had almost killed me a second time by shooting up Simone's apartment.

"No one got hurt there? Her parents?" he asked.

"No. Her father died a while back and her mother is always travelling. She lives with Niurka, the housekeeper, but she'd gone out to run errands when everything happened."

"We'll check on the housekeeper right away and also notify Simone's mother," Brother Gregorio said, his face emotionless.

My stomach churned, and it felt like I was going to throw up any second. I couldn't believe that other people might have been hurt because of me. I should never have gone to Simone's house.

"What's her mother's name?"

"Sarah Bimington."

Brother Gregorio raised his eyebrows in surprise. "The financier?"

I nodded. Apparently, I was one of the few people in the world who did not recognize the name when first told who Simone's mother was. Even an old monk knew about her. Maybe that was why I was one of Simone's only friends . . . I hadn't known enough to be impressed by who she was.

"Brother Gregorio, can you please tell me what's going on?" I asked.

He leaned back in his chair. "What I'm about to tell you is a secret of the highest order. People have died protecting this knowledge." He stayed quiet for a moment, evaluating me. "There are people at the highest levels of power who will do anything they can to learn what I'm going to tell you, so you need to understand that."

I nodded. My father had apparently become involved with something very big.

"I'll begin with the Hastati." He paused as if searching for the right words. "They're a secret organization that for almost two thousand years has been entrusted with one important duty—to protect the spear."

"A spear?" I asked, thinking I must have misunderstood.

"Not just any spear. You've heard of the Holy Lance of Longinus?"

I shook my head.

"Also known as the Spear of Destiny."

I gave him a blank stare.

Brother Gregorio let out a deep sigh. "Well, it was the spear carried by the Roman soldier Longinus, before he converted to Christianity. Next time you visit the Vatican, look in the alcove to the right of the altar. There is a large statue of Longinus with his spear there. He used that spear to stab Jesus on the cross at Golgotha, and the tip of it was imbued with, how should I say this? Mystical properties."

"You're kidding, right?" It sounded ridiculous. "A magic spear?"

Brother Gregorio narrowed his eyes. "I'm most certainly not kidding. The things that have happened to you today should tell you that this is no joke."

I swallowed the lump in my throat. His tone had suddenly turned more menacing. I decided to go along with his story, no matter how far-fetched it was.

"Okay, but what do you mean it has 'mystical properties'?"

The hardened look on his face softened a bit as he resumed his explanation. "The spear can control—no, let me rephrase, it can shape destiny. Leaders, like Charlemagne and Constantine, used it to win battles, to alter the world's path."

He paused, allowing his words to sink in. But they weren't. They were bouncing off me because it was all crazy talk.

He kept going. "The Hastati Council was in charge of the spear. They kept it safe and decided which events should be influenced. However, there were problems: There was always someone who wanted this power and would do anything to acquire it—like during World War Two. Hitler was able to find the spear and steal it." Brother Gregorio sighed. "Those were dark days, but the Hastati eventually got it back."

"So the spear is a bad thing?"

"No. The spearhead is only an object. It's neither good nor bad. It depends on how it is used to shape destiny."

"And Hitler used it to shape World War Two?" I couldn't believe I was actually listening to all this.

"No, no. Altering destiny on a wide scale is too difficult for even the most trained person to control. However, smaller events can be changed. Hitler probably influenced certain battles just as Charlemagne and Constantine did, but that is sometimes all it takes. Knowing which move to make, and at what time, can win the game. It's like knocking over the first domino and starting a big chain reaction. It all depends on the choices you make."

"Choices determine destiny," I muttered, thinking back to the gypsy woman's words.

"What's that?" Brother Gregorio asked.

"Nothing."

I leaned back in the chair, my arms crossed. I was sure my body language screamed out my disbelief of the whole thing.

"Ok-a-a-y, even if all this is true, I still don't see what that has to do with me."

Brother Gregorio smiled with the patience of a preschool teacher explaining the concept of numbers for the first time. "I'm getting to that. You see, while the Hastati were able to get the spear back, after seeing the emergence of nuclear powers during the Cold War and then the rise of global terrorism, a decision was made that the spearhead had to be permanently removed from society. What if it fell into the wrong hands? It was too risky. The spear was to be hidden in a remote and secret location. The plan was to have no one access those powers ever again."

"So, if the spear is hidden away, what's the problem?"

"The problem is that it was stolen before the Hastati could hide it."

I raised my eyebrows and shook my head incredulously. "The Hastati aren't very good at keeping it in the right hands, are they?"

Brother Gregorio's eyes narrowed and his jaw tightened. "True Hastati would give up their life for the spear," he said. "But every group has its bad apple. Their own personal Judas."

I hadn't meant to insult him. I leaned forward and tried to appear to be more receptive. "So where is it now?"

"No one knows. But at least it hasn't been used."

That made no sense. *Why would someone steal it and then not use it?* "How do you know?"

Brother Gregorio rubbed the back of his neck. "Let's just say the Hastati have taken measures to prevent it from being used, but that won't last much longer. Soon the power of the spear will become available again, and the Hastati believe they have to prevent it from being used by the wrong person. Just imagine if a madman, this one with nuclear weapons, got ahold of it."

"And the Hastati are after me because they think I know where it is?"

"Not exactly." He pressed his lips together before continuing. "After searching for it for years, the Council decided that if they could no longer protect the spear, then they would protect the world from the power of the spear."

"Uh-huh." I wished Simone were hearing this, because she was never going to believe me. "But that still doesn't explain why the Hastati are after me. I don't have it. I've never even heard of the thing."

"No, my dear." Brother Gregorio leaned forward and lowered his voice as if someone outside the small, messy room might hear the secret he was about to reveal. "It has everything to do with you. Cassandra, *you* are what makes the spearhead work."

—EIGHT—

Normally, there was no way I would believe any of what this strange old man was saying, but nothing about the day had been normal. *Did he think I was some kind of chosen one?* I tried to remain stone-faced, ignoring the urge to laugh. I wasn't special in any way. He had to have me confused with someone else.

"I know it's difficult to understand," he continued. "But it's in your blood."

"Type O?"

Brother Gregorio chuckled. "No, but that is a sign that you are one of them."

He made me sound like I was an alien.

"A true descendant of Saint Longinus," he continued. "One of the last to carry the mark of the spear."

Instinctively, I touched the palm-sized birthmark on my rib cage. Whenever I complained about how ugly it was, my father would tell me the mark reminded him of a Christmas tree. I was his greatest gift, he would say, and perfect.

Brother Gregorio nodded. "Yes, I believe Felipe told me it was on your right side." He studied me. "You, my dear Cassandra, are one of the last people who can access the spear's power. Not many in the Longinus line have both the mark and the correct blood type . . . Type O."

The nausea was coming back, and my expression probably showed it. I was just an average girl. Things like this were not supposed to happen to people like me. The palette of my life's painting was gray or maybe a boring variety of beige, not psychedelic neon. "No, there's got to be a mistake," I said.

"There's no mistake. You were born for this."

It was taking every ounce of self-control I had not to bolt out of the chair and run from the room. Could I grab Simone and get out the triple-locked door before Asher stopped us?

Brother Gregorio reached for a book on a shelf and wiped the dust off the spine with the sleeve of his brown robe. "Here." He opened the book and flipped to a dog-eared page. "In these ancient writings it speaks about how if the marked descendant is ever united with the spearhead, the powers would be unleashed and the gift of seeing different paths would be imparted."

"Uh-huh. But what does that mean exactly?" I asked, humoring him. I leaned forward to look at a picture of a yellowed scroll with strange lettering all over it.

"It means that with the spearhead, and some proper training, you'd be able to see different scenarios for events you want to influence and you could choose which one to follow. No one except a marked descendant can do that. There are only a handful of you born every generation."

"So there are others," I said, happy to hear that I wasn't alone.

"There used to be."

"Oh." I swallowed the lump in my throat.

"Cassandra, you have to understand. For anyone else the spearhead is just a sharp piece of metal. It holds no power. But with a marked descendant, it's different. One descendant at a time can access the power and become bound to it for life."

"Bound?" I thought back to the line in the old notebook. *The Guardian will be bound for life once the spearhead is used.*

"Yes. The power can only be accessed by a single marked descendant at a time. Once the spearhead is used, no one— not even another marked descendant—can use it until . . ."

"Until?"

Brother Gregorio leaned back in his chair. "Until that person dies. Once the bound descendant dies, the power becomes dormant until another marked descendant is united with the spearhead."

"And this power, it's dormant right now?"

A pained expression crossed the old monk's face. "Not exactly." He adjusted his robe. "Remember how I mentioned that the Hastati have taken action to make sure no one uses the spear? Well, a man named Tobias is still bound to the spear, but he has been in a coma for many years and isn't doing well." Brother Gregorio sighed. "When he dies, the power will be up for grabs by any marked descendant who comes in contact with the spear."

"But maybe someone good will get the power. Why do the Hastati have to control it?"

"It's too much power. Even Tobias became corrupted." He paused and looked away for moment. "You have to understand, Tobias was at one time very well respected among the Hastati . . . he was a good man. But something happened to him. He kept using the spear . . . he became obsessed with the idea that he could make the world a better place."

"What's wrong with that?" I could tell there was more to the story.

"Everything. He eventually decided that the only way to save the world was by destroying it and starting over. He thought that if he eliminated most people on earth, then we'd return to a more peaceful existence. A fresh start, he'd say."

"Wow." This was some major, delusional stuff. "He sounds crazy."

"Yes, well . . . like I said before, the power can be consuming." He took a deep breath. "And now, despite everyone's best efforts, it appears that he will soon die and the spear's power will become available again. That's why you are so valuable and why the Hastati can't risk having you fall into the wrong hands."

"So they'd rather just have me killed even if they wouldn't kill crazy Tobias?"

Brother Gregorio gave me a slight nod. "But don't worry, you are safe here. As long as you're within these walls, you will receive sanctuary and the Hastati will not harm you." He reached into a drawer, pulled out a small box, and slid it toward me. "But you must wear this at all times. You must never take it off."

Inside the box was an antique silver ring that looked a lot like the one I'd seen Asher wearing. Lifting it up, I noticed that the left side was etched with a spear, the right had a goblet, and in the middle was a shiny black stone.

"Why? Is there something magical about it?"

"It's more like insurance. Something to give me peace of mind, and in exchange I will grant you protection from the Hastati while you are here. It is not much to ask. But you have to promise to keep it on." He waited for me to answer.

"Sure." I slipped it over my finger, thinking I could always take it off later. "This is like the one Asher wears," I said. "That must mean he is being protected also."

"You noticed." Brother Gregorio smiled. "You are very observant for one so young." He paused. "He wears his for other reasons. But for you, it will keep you out of harm's way."

I didn't like the idea of depending on an old monk and strange jewelry to keep me safe. "Can't I just move back to the US after you find my father? Disappear over there." I twisted the ring around my finger.

"There is no disappearing when it comes to the Hastati. Their reach goes to the highest levels of power throughout the world, and they have people who can harm you everywhere. You are only safe in a few places."

"But how can you know for sure?" I tugged on the ring, but it didn't budge.

"I used to be Hastati, and I can assure you that they will respect the confines of this place. And your father"—he crinkled his eyes as he stared straight at me—"I know he would want you safe. So you will stay here and wear the ring."

"I guess," I muttered.

"This is not a game, Cassandra. You must not leave. You would be in danger anywhere else." He closed the books on his desk and heaved everything back on the shelves.

"So basically, I'm a prisoner." The ring was feeling more like a handcuff.

"No, no. Of course not. You are free to go elsewhere, but I can't guarantee your safety anywhere but here." Brother Gregorio leaned back to observe me. "I can see the fire in your eyes, Cassandra. Smoldering just beneath the surface. It reminds me of . . ." He didn't finish the sentence.

"My father?" I asked, although up until today I'd always thought of him as cautious and careful. Definitely an artist who painted his life with muted colors.

"Well, yes. I do believe I see a little of him in you." He adjusted the top of his brown robe. "Felipe was . . . is . . . such a determined man. You know he's been searching for the spear for years in order to exchange it for your safety. And I think he was close to finding it."

My hand skimmed over the top of my messenger bag. Inside was one of the notebooks my father had given me. Was there information about the location of the spear inside? I wanted to pull it out and read it, but I wasn't sure if this was something I should share with Brother Gregorio. Maybe it was better to talk it over with Simone first.

Brother Gregorio was watching me carefully. "Are you sure Felipe didn't mention anything else?" he asked, his fingers laced and resting over his large belly.

I hesitated for a moment before speaking. "Actually, there was something."

Brother Gregorio leaned forward. "Yes?"

"Well, right after my father got shot he did give me this old notebook . . . written in Latin and some other languages. I recognized the word Hastati and it talked about a Guardian being bound for life."

Brother Gregorio straightened up. "The Guardian's Journal?" His voice became more excited. "He found it? Let me see."

"I don't know. It might be that. It's just . . . there's a problem." I bit my lip, hating to admit my own mistake, but thinking that Brother Gregorio might help get the book. "In all the craziness at Simone's apartment, it got left behind."

The old monk's shoulders dropped. "Fine, I will see what we can do to get it back."

He shuffled toward the door and then paused. He looked back at me still sitting motionless in the chair. "Cassandra, are you all right?"

I moved my hand away from the messenger bag and stayed quiet about the other notebook. My father's warning not to trust anyone echoed in my brain. For now, that would have to include Brother Gregorio.

I nodded and slowly got up.

"I know this is a lot to take in, but I will have Asher show you to your room, where you can rest and gather your thoughts. In the meantime, I will try my best to find Felipe and the Guardian's Journal. Just be patient." He gave me the slightest smile, the tip of his beard shifting as the corners of his mouth went up. "Asher and I will find him, Cassandra . . . and eventually the spear."

I chewed on the inside of my cheek. "How does finding the spear help me?" I asked.

"Because once the Hastati Council has the spear, then they will have no reason to come after you or any of the marked ones. The Hastati aren't monsters . . . just misguided people who are trying to protect the world from a greater evil. Sacrificing a few for the benefit of many. It's nothing personal."

My dad had been shot, there were assassins everywhere in the world trying to kill me, and yet this guy expected me to sit around and wait for things to get better?

Brother Gregorio was wrong. This was completely personal. And that meant I had to come up with my own plan.

—NINE—

Asher walked a few paces ahead of me, and Simone trailed behind both of us. We were on the second floor in the open-air breezeway with the lush garden down below. The walls, made of old stone blocks, were bare except for the occasional tapestry that seemed to date back to the Middle Ages and a few portraits of various saints being martyred in one fashion or another.

"So are you going to tell me what the old guy said?" Simone whispered, having caught up to me. "And what's with the new jewelry?"

I pulled on the ring to show her, but found myself unable to get it off. "I'll tell you," I said, motioning over to Asher. "When we're alone."

"Fine, but do you really think we'll be safe here?" She gazed up at the twilit sky above. "I mean, it's not like there are armed guards surrounding the place."

"If he says you're safe, then you are," Asher answered without turning around or breaking his stride.

"Wow, nice eavesdropping," Simone muttered, but Asher didn't respond. "Is this real?" she asked, pausing in front of one of the paintings that had caught her eye.

"A real Caravaggio? It can't be." I stopped in front of the dark, gruesome painting of Salome with the head of John the Baptist on a platter.

"Why not?" Asher questioned me. "Not all of Caravaggio's paintings are in museums."

I got closer to the canvas and pointed to Salome's dress. "I know that, but the strokes right here . . . they're uneven. See?"

Asher pursed his lips as if noticing the fault for the first time.

"What about this one?" Asher walked over to another painting.

I studied the painting of an old man. "Hm, looks like a pretty decent copy of a Tiziano."

"Interesting." Asher smiled. "You called him Tiziano and not Titian like most people. You do know your art, Cassandra."

"My dad is an art history professor, so some of it is bound to rub off on me," I explained. "And call me Cassie. Everyone does."

"Art nerds unite," Simone said, loud enough for us to hear even though she was still staring at the painting of Salome. "So none of this is real art?" she remarked as she made her way back to us. "They're all fakes."

"Well, it's real art." Asher tensed up. "Just not the original masterpieces."

Something about how he said the words *real art* stood out. "Did you paint them?" I touched the corner of the gold frame around the Tiziano look-alike.

Asher pulled at the collar of his gray polo, stretching it out around his Adam's apple. He stuck his hands in his jeans, shifted his weight from foot to foot, and gave me a slight nod.

"They're really good," I said, admiring the skill it had taken to make the paintings. "A strong balance between light and dark. My dad always says that's the key."

"Thanks."

Simone cleared her throat. "Can we finish up the art tour a little later?"

"Certainly," Asher said through clenched teeth and a fake smile. He walked a few more steps and opened a large door made of heavy wooden planks held together by a slender iron plate that wrapped around the top and bottom. "This is your room, Cassie." He held the door back and turned on the chandelier.

The room itself was larger than I expected and it looked like a mix of medieval and modern with an old-style canopy bed across from a flat-screen TV.

Simone walked over to one of two narrow windows, pulled aside the large red velvet curtains that draped to the floor, and peered out.

"Not much of a view," she commented. I could see the wall of the neighboring building from where I stood.

"Mm-hm." Asher pointed at the bed. "That's yours, and I put a fold-up cot next to it since you brought . . . *company*." He opened a narrow door in the corner. "This is your private bathroom, and there is a small suitcase with some of your clothes next to that chest of drawers."

I almost didn't hear him. My attention was drawn to the small nightstand that had a framed photo of my father and me that we took when we first moved to Rome. "Wait." I spun around to face him. "How did you get that picture? And my clothes?"

Asher shrugged. "I'm guessing your father sent them over." He paused. "You didn't know?"

"Of course she didn't know," Simone called out from across the room. "Why do you think she's asking?"

Asher's eyes locked with mine. I felt like he was trying to read me . . . to make some connection. But there was no way I was going to reveal anything to someone I'd just met. I stared blankly right back at him.

"By the way, what exactly do you do here, Asher?" Simone asked. "Are you like the help or something?"

Asher pulled away from our staring contest. "No. I'm not the help," he said dryly. "What's *your* purpose here?" He chuckled. "Oh, right, you don't have one."

Simone's eyes blazed with pent-up anger.

"I think you should go now," I said to Asher.

"Yes, go." Simone dismissively waved him off. "Now."

Asher hesitated for a moment. "Cassie, if you need anything, just let me know. I'll be down the hall."

"She needs to find her father. Can you help her with *that*?" Simone raised one of her perfectly arched eyebrows and, before he could reply, she added, "Didn't think so."

An uneasy silence hung in the air.

I stood motionless; my thoughts were flying in different directions. How long had my father known I'd be coming here, and when had he planned to tell me? Did he plan on just dumping me here while he went off to hunt for the spear? Where was he right now? Was he alive or . . . no, I couldn't even think of the alternative. I just needed to find him and that spear thing. I could set things straight just like he was planning to do by returning it to the Hastati. Then, if what Brother Gregorio said was true, they'd leave us alone.

"Earth to Cassie, come in, Cassie."

"Huh?" I said, noticing that Simone was now sitting in a wingback chair by the bed and that Asher was gone.

"You were staring off into space."

"Oh, yeah. Just thinking."

"So-o-o-o . . . we're alone. Are you going to give me a hint to what's going on?"

"Hold on," I said, making sure no one was in the breeze-way before closing the door.

Simone sat on the edge of her seat . . . literally. Another inch and she'd fall off and hit the floor. I plopped down on the bed, which creaked with my every move.

"It's all pretty bizarre, so just go with it, okay?"

Simone nodded.

"No snide remarks or comments until I tell you everything?"

"When have I—?" Simone stopped herself as I cocked my head to the side and gave her a look.

"Fine." She pretended to lock her mouth and throw away the key.

I told her everything I could remember. Not holding back on any detail. By the end, for the first time in all the months I'd known her, Simone appeared dumbfounded.

"Well?" I asked. "What do you think? Crazy, right? But the weird thing is that I kinda believe it. All of it."

Simone slowly nodded.

"You can talk now." I waited.

Nothing.

"Seriously, say something. Even if it's 'I'm out of here.' I need to know what you're thinking."

She stared at me as if we'd just met.

"So you're supposed to be like a superhero or something," she said.

This was what she was thinking? "No, no. I think it's more like a recessive gene that pops up out of nowhere. Like having eyes that are two different colors."

"No. This is more than that." Simone bit the edge of her nail. "If you connect with the spear, you can do stuff like control the future, right? And there are people who want to kill you to make sure you don't do that. That's pretty much a superpower."

"Nah, you know me, I'm not superhero material." I hesitated before saying the next sentence, but it had to be done. "But, you are right about the being-hunted thing. I think you should probably go. It really isn't safe to be around me."

"No way!" She shook her head. "I'm not leaving you here with two strangers and some goofy ring to keep you safe. Besides, don't you find it weird that the bearded monk lives here like a hermit with a young guy and no one else?"

66

"Maybe Asher is a monk-in-training or something."

"Doesn't look like any monk I've ever seen. Plus, he could be a creeper. There are good-looking and charming sociopaths out there, you know. So, as long as you're here, I'm here."

"Yeah, well, I'm thinking of not being here, either. I want to go out and find the spear on my own."

Simone stopped chewing her fingernail. "Really? Even though you'd be a huge target the moment you leave? You'd take that risk?"

"I have to . . . it's my dad," I said. "Plus, the Hastati don't have to know that I've left. And don't the self-defense people always say that it's harder to hit a moving target? Staying here makes me a sitting duck, no matter what Brother Gregorio says."

"Hm." I could see Simone considering the pros and cons of my idea. "And that was your dad's plan, right? To find the spear and trade it in for your safety."

"I think so."

"We'd have to know where to look. We can't leave without a plan."

"We?" I hadn't planned on Simone wanting to go with me.

"Well, yeah." She smiled. "Someone has to watch your back. So any ideas on where to start?"

"I'm hoping there's something in this notebook my dad gave me." I pulled it out of my small messenger bag.

"How about Brother G—think he can help?"

"I don't think he wants us to know too much. Plus, I don't know how much I trust him. He said he used to be Hastati—what if he turns us over to them?" I flipped through the pages of the journal. Many of them had detailed drawings of paintings or buildings, while others had random names and dates. I immediately recognized the familiar, elegant handwriting of my father. "It's written in Spanish," I mumbled, turning over several pages that he had crossed out with a big X.

A dull ache formed in my chest as I thought of the countless times my father had insisted I practice my Spanish. Always telling me that if he could learn English after arriving in America on a raft from Cuba as a young man, then I should be able to learn Spanish from the comfort of whatever nice suburban home we were renting at the time.

"So?" Simone commented as I stared at the first page, lost in thought. "I thought you spoke English and Spanish."

"I do, kinda." I let out a sigh. "It's just . . . my dad wrote this."

"But that's good!" She sat next to me on the bed. The springs underneath us squeaked from the added weight. "That means we'll know what he was thinking. Didn't Brother Gregorio say he was close to finding the spear? Go to the last page," Simone suggested, peering over my shoulder. "See what his last words were."

I knew she didn't mean it was the last thing my father would ever write, but it felt ominous nonetheless. I flipped about two-thirds through the small journal and found his last entry. The only thing written was:

En la ciudad que se está muriendo, nadie recibe el secreto hasta que el hombre que nadie ve contesta la pregunta.

My father had circled the quote several times and drawn little question marks around it. Then, underneath, he had written *CDB* with a big exclamation mark.

"In the city that is dying, no one receives the secret until the man that no one sees answers the question," I said out loud, translating the quote to English.

"Does that mean anything to you?" Simone asked me. "Is it some kind of riddle?"

I shook my head. "I have no idea. Might be an old Cuban saying or something. I don't know."

"What about 'CDB'? Somebody's initials?"

"No clue," I said and flipped back to the beginning of the journal. There were descriptions of paintings that I knew he had studied or lectured about in his classes, but I didn't know what any of it meant. Some of it corresponded to places we'd lived, but most of it meant nothing to me. I saw Brother Gregorio's name and address in one of the middle pages, and the next-to-last page had a list of items like he was planning to go on a trip.

"What was he *doing*?" I said to myself.

"What did you say?"

I looked up at Simone and saw her cell phone was in her hand. "Why do you have that out? I told you they might track us."

"They probably know we're here by now. Plus, didn't the monk tell you that there was some kind of truce or magic force field with that ring where they can't get us in here?" She stuffed the phone back into her jeans. "Doesn't matter anyway. There's no cell phone signal and the Wi-Fi is locked." She walked back to me. "But we should try to look up the dying-city thing when we find a computer. They have to have one if they have secure Wi-Fi."

"And I just thought of another problem." I dumped everything from my bag. A lip gloss, the two fake passports, a few pens, a pack of gum, and my wallet scattered across the bed. "What do we do when we figure out where we want to go? You don't have a purse, and all I have is about twenty euros. That won't get us very far."

"I can take care of that." Simone cocked her head to the side. "Being Sarah Bimington's daughter does have its perks, you know. I just need to make a couple of calls for things to happen."

"Are you sure you want to do that? It's still not too late to bail. I won't be upset. It would probably make more sense if you did."

"Don't ask me that anymore. I'm not leaving . . . especially since I now know why I'm here."

"You do?"

"Yeah, even if it's not exactly what I'd imagined." She gave me a wink. "Every hero needs a sidekick."

—TEN—

A best friend. Everyone deserved one, but I never thought I'd get one. I'd spent most of my life moving from one American college town to another, meeting new groups of kids at every stop. At first I convinced myself that they were all my friends, but eventually I figured out that the moment I was gone, so was their memory of me. It was all just temporary, because I was only passing through. I'd decided that real friends were for other people, until I met Simone. We became inseparable from the day when Latchke railed on her for not having turned in an assignment, and I pointed out that I'd seen him drop several papers earlier in the hallway. Simone had jumped on that idea, saying he could've lost her assignment, and we turned the tables on him. Later, I came to find out that Simone had never done the assignment, but by then a friend-ship had been formed.

Now it was because of Simone that I felt like this was something I could handle.

"We should shower and change. Get the grime from the tunnel off of us before we keep going," Simone suggested, holding one of the shirts my dad had packed for me.

"We do smell a little rancid." I thought about the putrid water that had splashed all over the bottom of my jeans. Yes, feeling clean with new clothes might even help us come up with fresh ideas about what to do next. "Just grab whatever clothes you think might fit . . . although the pants will be short on you. I'll go after you're done."

"Okay. I won't take long," Simone said, slipping into the bathroom. I got comfortable on the bed and turned on the TV, since I knew Simone would be a while. She always took forever to get ready.

I watched the news, hoping that there might be some information about the shooting or my dad, but there was nothing.

By the time the sports reporter finished giving the latest soccer scores, there was a knock at the door. I quickly shoved my father's journal under the mattress.

"Cassie?" It was Asher. "Dinner will be ready in about half an hour."

"Okay, sure," I called out. "We'll meet you down there."

A few minutes later Simone came out of the bathroom, wearing my T-shirt and a pair of jeans that looked like capris. Her hair was wrapped in a towel.

"See, I didn't take too long." She pointed to the TV. "Anything about them shooting up my house?"

I had completely forgotten that an attack on Sarah Bimington's house would be a much more newsworthy event than my dad's shooting, but it hadn't been covered, either. "No . . . nothing." I looked at the small alarm clock on the night table. "And thirty-four minutes isn't exactly fast."

"It is for me." She plopped down on the bed. "You should try taking a long shower. It helps you think."

"Yeah, maybe." I shrugged, feeling exhausted. "They want us downstairs for dinner in a little bit . . . although I can't even think about food right now." I hugged the pillow. "I just feel like curling up on this bed, going to sleep, and waking up tomorrow to find out that this was all some crazy nightmare."

"Well, unfortunately, I don't think that's going to happen."

"I know," I said and slid off the bed for my turn in the bathroom.

By the time I finished, I had a renewed sense of energy. Simone had been right about the shower. It not only made me feel refreshed, but I felt more focused. It was obvious that we needed more information before we could set up a plan to get the spear, and that meant we needed to do some investigating into the dying city.

"Ready to get some answers?" I asked, combing through my wet hair as Simone shut off the hairdryer.

"Let's go see what Mr. Junior Monk can tell us."

Leaving the bedroom, Simone and I stepped into the breezeway, which was now lit by sconces with lightbulbs that mimicked flickering candles. The interior courtyard had grown dark with nightfall.

"This place is a little creepy," I whispered to Simone as we approached the stairs.

The monastery was the type of place that might have a dungeon or a secret lab. I was about to make a joke about Asher being an improvement over Dr. Frankenstein's Igor when I spotted him rounding the corner.

"Dinner's almost ready," he told us. "Zio wanted me to come up and get you."

"Zio? As in uncle?" I asked. "You're Brother Gregorio's nephew?"

"Yeah, guess I should have mentioned that before."

I exchanged a quick look with Simone. This answered one question. He wasn't a monk-in-training; he was family.

We cut through the courtyard garden to get to the kitchen and dining rooms.

"So, have you lived here long?" I asked, initiating phase one of my plan—information gathering.

"About five years, since I was ten. Zio . . . Brother Gregorio . . . took me in after my parents passed away."

"Oh." I glanced at Simone, not knowing what else to say after that.

"Anyone else live here?" Simone asked.

Asher shook his head. "Nope. Just my uncle and me."

"So do you go to school around here?" Simone asked, stopping to look at a marble bust propped on top of a stone pillar.

"No," he answered.

"Isn't that a little strange? Just staying here with your uncle all the time." Simone was like a newspaper reporter digging for facts. "Don't you want to go to school?"

"No. Yes." He took a deep breath and started over. "I mean, it's not strange, and I already go to school . . . online." Asher's jaw squared out a bit. "What's with all the questions anyway?"

"Nothing." I shrugged. "Just curious and trying to sort things out. Get to know where we are."

Asher's shoulders relaxed. "Yeah, I guess it is pretty overwhelming."

"You said you study online," Simone called out, her face only an inch away from the pillar, as she'd gotten closer to read the bronze plaque hidden in the shadows. "Can we use your computer?"

Asher reached for the handle of the door that led directly into the dining room. "I don't know if you're allowed to go online. I'll have to ask my uncle."

"Of course you do." Simone rolled her eyes as she walked over to us. "Heaven forbid you just say yes."

"You don't get it." Asher opened the door. "And you never will. This is bigger than you imagine."

"Oh, I can imagine pretty big things." Simone squeezed between the two of us. "Unlike boys who've been locked up in a monastery . . . I get out."

"Hey," Asher said. "You don't know anything about me. I go out plenty like any normal guy."

"Yeah, really normal." Simone shook her head and walked into the dining room.

It was obvious that Asher wanted to say something, but he didn't. He just stood there. I placed a hand on his arm. I wanted more information.

"Listen, she didn't mean anything. She's just stressed. You're lucky to have Brother Gregorio; he seems very nice." Asher stayed still, his muscles tensed while his eyes tracked Simone through the French doors as she walked from the dining room to the kitchen. "My mother passed away when

I was little, so I understand how important it is to have someone," I said.

"I know. You were just a baby." He was still glaring at Simone, silent darts shooting from his eyes through the glass doors.

"Wait, what?" I pulled away from him. "You know about my mom?"

"Huh?" Asher snapped back into the present and looked at me, confused.

"You said you knew my mother had died. What else do you know about me?"

"Not much. Just that you and your dad moved to Rome a little while ago. That you have the birthmark, basic stuff like that."

I stayed quiet. There was nothing basic about this information. He probably knew more about what was happening with me than I did.

Asher fidgeted with his hoodie's zipper. "We should go in and have dinner. Zio doesn't like the food to get cold." He took a step toward the open door.

"Wait." I stretched my arm across the doorway, blocking him. "Just tell me something." I flashed him my ring. "Why do you have to wear one like this? Do you have a birthmark, too?"

"What did Zio tell you?" he replied.

"He didn't say anything. That's why I'm asking you."

Asher looked unsure of what to do next. His eyes darted

over to the dining room, then back to me. "I wear it because it's my duty."

"What does that mean?"

He unhooked my fingers from the doorframe. "My family has always been there to protect and serve. It's what we do."

"Protect and serve? Like a cop?"

"Something like that." He pointed to Brother Gregorio walking back from the kitchen with Simone. "We should go in. He might have information about your father."

If he was trying to distract me, it worked. At the mention of my father, all other questions faded to the background. I needed to know if he'd been found.

"This isn't over," I said, walking into the brightly lit dining room.

"It hasn't even started," Asher answered.

—ELEVEN—

"Cassandra," Brother Gregorio greeted me as I walked into the room. "I was just telling Simone that I prepared my famous pasta fagioli soup and some lamb chops for dinner."

"Thank you," I said, not terribly interested in the menu, "but were you able to find out anything about my father or Niurka?"

"The housekeeper is fine. She wasn't even there when the shooting happened."

I let out a sigh of relief. At least that was one person I hadn't put in danger.

"Unfortunately, I don't have news yet on your father, but I hope to hear something soon. I've made some calls." He shuffled over to one of the rustic wooden chairs and pulled it out for Simone.

"Thank you," Simone said, taking her seat.

I stayed standing. "But was he at the hospital? Why wouldn't they give me information?" I asked, throwing away my plan to play it cool.

"I'm not sure. We'll find out more shortly." Brother Gregorio motioned for Asher to pull back my chair. "Have a seat."

"I got it," I said, pushing Asher's hand out of the way and pulling out my own chair.

Brother Gregorio's bushy gray eyebrows twitched as he glanced over at Asher, who shrugged in response.

"I'm afraid we don't have much information on the journal that was left behind, either." Brother Gregorio ladled some soup into a bowl and passed it to me. "Asher couldn't find it when he went by a little while ago."

"Hold on," Simone interrupted. "He was inside my house?"

"Nice place," Asher replied. "Like museum meets cheap world bazaar."

"Was Niurka there? Maybe she has it," I suggested, unable to hide my disappointment at having lost such a valuable clue.

Simone was still fixated on the fact that Asher had been inside her house. "I'll have you know that everything I own is legit and expensive," she retorted. "My mother sends back only the finest things from her trips."

Asher had a look of satisfaction at having gotten under Simone's skin. "If you say so." He faced me. "And the housekeeper was there, but said she hadn't seen it."

"We made sure the police listed the entire thing as random vandalism so as not to bring any more attention to the matter." Brother Gregorio stopped for a moment, silently praying over his food before he continued speaking. "Of course, I contacted your mother, Simone. I explained that your house had been attacked, but that you were safe at the monastery. However, she'd still like to speak with you. You can call her after dinner from the house phone."

"Wasn't she worried about me? I mean, freaked out or anything?"

"Of course she was concerned, but she considers you very

self-reliant. She seemed reassured to hear that I was affiliated with your school and that I'd make sure your absence is excused."

Simone's shoulders dropped a little.

"You said you're affiliated with our school. How?" I asked.

"Let's just say I have some friends there," said Brother Gregorio.

"And yet Asher doesn't attend," Simone mused. "Interesting."

"This is where I need to be." Asher made no eye contact with anyone, but instead focused on his soup.

"But why are you here, Asher? Who are you here to protect?" I asked, hoping that every small revelation would get me closer to the answers I needed.

Brother Gregorio wiped the edges of his beard, near the corners of his mouth, with a napkin before motioning toward Simone. "Cassandra, as I explained earlier, some matters are private and require—"

I leaned back in the chair and crossed my arms. "Brother Gregorio, I appreciate all you're doing for me, really I do, but Simone knows everything. There's no need to keep secrets when I'll just tell her later."

Simone rolled her shoulders back, a victorious twinkle in her eye.

"Ridiculous," Asher exclaimed, dropping his spoon in disgust. Just then, the phone rang. "I'll get it," he announced, thrusting his chair back and storming out toward the living room.

"My nephew is still learning to control his emotions," Brother Gregorio commented after Asher left the room. "You'll have to forgive him. But you do need to understand something. The Hastati value secrecy above all else. If anyone else learns of this, you are putting them and your father in danger. There can be no loose ends. Even the existence of the Hastati is shrouded in mystery."

A heavy silence filled the room. I hadn't meant to put Simone in more danger.

"But what's done is done." Brother Gregorio took a sip of water. "If you have revealed to Simone what I have told you, I suppose I will have to find a ring for her to wear as well. I will get one tomorrow."

"I'm not wearing it," Simone said matter-of-factly.

Brother Gregorio's eyes narrowed, and he gave Simone a cold, hard stare. "My dear, I did not ask."

"Zio." Asher rushed in from the other room. "It's for you. They said the password."

Brother Gregorio immediately stood up, his large belly hitting the table, jostling all the water glasses. "Yes, yes." He moved as fast as he could, though it didn't seem like his three-hundred-pound body would cooperate with anything more than a snail's pace. He left the room, and Asher stood in the archway.

Simone and I glanced at each other. There was no way I was going to sit and wait. We both jumped up at the same time and went straight for Asher.

"Brother Gregorio needs privacy," he said, holding out his arms to block the entrance to the living room.

"How do you know that?" Simone narrowed her eyes. "He didn't say anything."

"It's probably something to do with me or my dad. I have a right to hear it," I added.

"Just stay here. He'll let us know if—"

Simone shoved Asher, causing him to lose his balance and stumble. We were both about to rush through when he lunged forward, grabbed Simone by the arm, twisted it, and pushed her back into the dining room.

"Are you insane?" Simone yelled as Asher let her go and resumed blocking the archway. "How dare you grab me and—"

"Shhh!" I interrupted. I could hear Brother Gregorio from where we stood.

"I understand." Silence, followed by the old monk saying, "Yes, I agree that it is the best for all concerned. *Grazie*."

I couldn't take it anymore. I pushed against Asher's chest with all my might. He didn't budge; it was like pushing against a wall. For someone who didn't look to be that thick or muscular, he was very solid.

"Asher . . . please. It's about my dad," I begged softly, but it was too late. I heard the click of the phone just as Asher relented and stepped aside.

Brother Gregorio was waddling around the couch in the middle of the room. "Cassandra," he called out, but he didn't have to raise his voice much, because in an instant I was in front of him with Simone at my heels. "Your father . . ."

"Yes?" My heart pounded in my chest.

"He's alive. They were able to remove the bullet and it didn't hit any vital organs."

I turned and hugged Simone.

"But?" Simone asked, cutting off my celebration.

That's when I noticed Brother Gregorio's grim demeanor.

"After the surgery . . . he hasn't regained consciousness." Brother Gregorio took one of my hands in his. "Now, that isn't completely unheard of, especially after such a procedure."

I pulled away, not wanting to be consoled. "I want to go see him."

Brother Gregorio shook his head and began shuffling toward the dining room. "You can't, because I don't know where he is. He's been transferred somewhere to recover."

I chased after him. "You have to know. If he's not at the hospital, where is he? Don't lie to us!"

He spun quickly around. "My child, I don't lie."

"I didn't mean . . . I just . . . I want to see him. You can't keep us here forever."

"Cassandra, I know this is all very difficult for you." He put an arm around my shoulders. "You've only been here for a few hours, and you won't have to stay here forever . . . just until the spear is found and returned to the Hastati. It's what your father would want. Now come, let's finish our dinner and I'll tell you everything I was told."

There wasn't much I could do. He held all the cards. It was up to him to tell me anything or nothing.

Unfortunately, everything that Brother Gregorio knew added up to a bunch of nothing. He knew that my father had been rushed into surgery at the hospital where I had dropped him off, and then transferred to a different facility. Supposedly, the Hastati weren't interested in harming my father—they'd been aiming at *me*—but they didn't want him running around unsupervised, either. As for his whereabouts, they wouldn't tell Brother Gregorio anything, and that was by design. The less he knew, the less he could reveal to me or anyone else. Apparently, it was the way everything with the Hastati worked. It was the key to keeping the secret organization . . . secret.

I couldn't imagine leaving my father in the care of the same people who had shot him, but Brother Gregorio swore that he'd receive the absolute best treatment. That was hard to believe, because what kind of doctors work in a secret hospital? This all convinced me of one thing: The only way to help my father and have our lives go back to normal was for me to find the spear and find it fast.

—TWELVE—

"Did you hear all that?" Simone mumbled as she hung up the phone. After dinner, we'd retreated to the living room to make the call to Simone's mother. "Not even when she hears about an attack does she care how I'm feeling. She just wanted to know how you knew Brother Gregorio." Simone shook her head.

"She knows you're safe and that you can handle things on your own," I said, trying to be supportive. "And I think your answer about my dad and Brother Gregorio being friends was perfect. It wasn't even really a lie."

Simone scoffed. "Whatever. She couldn't even promise to come home soon. Said she'd try." She shrugged as if to forget the whole thing, but I knew how much it bothered her. I'd seen it before when her mother forgot to call on Simone's birthday or when she didn't come home for Christmas. Simone had even ended up spending her entire winter break sleeping over at my little apartment and, although she had all the money in the world, she'd sworn it was the best holiday she'd ever had.

"At least I did what she asked and called," Simone said. "She can't complain. Now, let's find that computer and figure out what your dad was talking about."

After we searched downstairs and found nothing, things started looking a little grim.

"In Tough Guy's room," Simone said, rushing up the stairs. "I bet he has it there."

"We can't just go in his room," I said, catching up to her.

"Sure we can." She leaned over the railing and pointed down to the first floor. "Check it out. He's still washing pots and pans. We won't get caught. We just have to be quick."

I bit my lip. Brother Gregorio and Asher had been nothing but nice to us. They seemed to actually be giving us some type of protection from the Hastati—at least, we hadn't been shot at in the past few hours—so we couldn't afford to get them angry at us. "Or we could just ask again."

"And risk Brother Gregorio saying no?" Simone shook her head. "I've learned that it's better to ask for forgiveness than for permission." She pushed open the first door, revealing a dark room.

"Fine." I relented and flicked on the light switch, which revealed nothing except a punching bag, a pull-up bar, and some weights in the corner.

"Check the next one." Simone motioned for me to go back outside.

I hurried down the hall. This room, unlike the first one, was bathed in moonlight coming in from two large windows. I could see drop cloths protecting the parquet floor, and there were easels with half-painted canvases scattered around the room. I paused to look at the different paintings, which were quite good, if a bit gruesome with their beheadings of different saints.

"Over here!" Simone said in a muted cry.

Quickly, I closed the door to the art studio and made my way to the room two doors from mine.

"He's ridiculously neat," Simone said as I stood in the doorway. "He even has his pencils lined up on the desk."

The room itself wasn't much different from my room, except his bed had an old brown-and-blue bedspread and there was a poster of a guy surfing a huge wave hanging on the wall.

Simone turned on the desk lamp and rummaged through each drawer. "The cord is here, but no laptop. See if it's over there," she said, pointing to an old armoire in the corner.

"This doesn't feel right." I glanced back down the breeze-way. "We really shouldn't do this."

Simone froze in midsearch and stared at me. "Fine, it's your call." She lifted up her hands like a thief being caught. "I just thought you wanted answers."

"I do." Simone was right. The old rules didn't apply any-more. Plus, we only wanted to use the computer; we weren't stealing anything. "Keep looking," I said, dashing across the room to open the large armoire. Jackets and pants were hang-ing inside, and the T-shirts were folded perfectly on the bottom, like in a store.

"Anything?" Simone had now moved on to a chest of drawers.

"No, but—"

"What are you doing in here?" Asher's voice bounced off the monastery walls.

I jumped, slamming shut the armoire door. "Um, we needed . . . I mean, we were only looking for—"

"There's nothing in here for you." He walked over to the chest of drawers and shoved the middle drawer shut. "This is my stuff."

Simone backed away toward the door. "We were just looking for a computer, and if you'd told us earlier where—"

"Here!" Asher yanked open a drawer in his nightstand and pulled out a laptop. "I was coming upstairs to get it for you anyway." He thrust the computer in my direction. "Knock yourselves out . . . in your own room."

I took the laptop and tried to explain. "I'm sorry, but we were desperate," I said. "We normally wouldn't have—"

"Just get out," he said, no emotion in his voice.

Simone waved me over.

"Sorry," I repeated as I walked out of the room.

Asher didn't reply, and he didn't look at me. He turned around and stared out the window.

We retreated to my room, and I immediately jumped onto the bed and flipped open the laptop. I was about to search for anything to do with dying cities when I noticed Simone dragging a large wingback chair toward the closed door.

"What are you doing?" I asked, typing my search for any references about dying cities into the computer.

She pushed the chair up and underneath the brass door handle. Then she let out a big sigh and leaned against the wall. "It's been a rough day and, well, we're in a creepy monastery with two weird guys inside and assassins on the outside. Call me crazy, but I'm not taking any chances."

She had a point. A very good one.

Simone scooted next to me on the bed and peered over my shoulder at the first few entries that popped up when I searched for dying cities. "Detroit? We're going to have to go to Detroit?"

I didn't say anything, but continued to read. I'd go anywhere to get back to my regular life and save my dad. I couldn't believe that twelve hours earlier I'd been sitting in class and my biggest worry had been how to survive another day of Latchke's lectures. It all seemed so long ago.

"There." I pointed to the bottom entry. It described an old Italian town nicknamed the Dying City, whose real name was Civita di Bagnoregio. "CDB!" I exclaimed, clicking on the link to get more information. What popped up was beautiful and, at the same time, a little scary. A current photo of the medieval-looking town showed it to be perched atop a narrow and steep plateau. There was a footbridge that crossed the huge gorge and rose dramatically to meet a winding road near the top.

"Figures it would be in a place like that," Simone muttered.

"Yeah." I nodded in agreement. "But it says it's only about a hundred and twenty kilometers from Rome. That isn't too far. We just need a car."

"I can take care of that." Simone snapped her fingers. "Done!"

"How? What are you going to do?"

"Does Batman ever ask Robin? Or Harry ask Hermione?" Simone answered. "Trust me."

I cocked my head to the side and waited.

Simone let out a long sigh. "I'm going to do what I do best. Use my mother's name to get us a driver and put it on her tab."

"Oh, well, yeah. That makes sense."

"Glad you approve." She smiled. "Now, what's next on the list?"

"Oh, I don't know. Make sure we don't get killed while we look for a mysterious spear that's been missing for who knows how long by finding a guy that no one's ever seen."

Simone pursed her lips and grimaced.

"It all sounds impossible," I said, falling back against the pillow.

"Difficult," Simone answered. "Not impossible. And the good thing is, no one expects us to go look for it."

I propped myself up on my elbows and stared at Simone. She was right. Assassins or not, this was the only way.

—THIRTEEN—

The early light of dawn was beginning to filter through the window when I came out of the bathroom. Simone was still asleep, the red bedspread pulled beneath her chin. "Wake up," I whispered, shaking her shoulder.

Simone stirred, then buried her head under the pillow. It hadn't taken much to convince her to let me sleep on the cot, but it was the least I could do. We'd stayed up late researching the spear, the Hastati, and the medieval city of Civita, but more importantly, we'd come up with a plan.

"Simone, come on." I sat on the foot of the bed. "The car is probably already outside."

"They'll wait," she mumbled, still not moving. "They always do."

I took a deep breath. Thanks to her, we had a driver to take us on the two-hour journey, but we needed to leave the monastery before anyone noticed. I looked at the small clock on the night table. "Simone, it's almost six. We really have to go."

She rubbed her eyes open. "I know, I know," she said, propping herself up on her elbows. "Give me three minutes, okay?"

"A real three minutes. Hurry." I grabbed a pen and pulled my father's journal from under the mattress. Ripping out a blank page from the back, I thought about what to write to

Brother Gregorio. It would have to be a "thank you, but no thank you" type of note.

Short and simple.

> *Brother Gregorio,*
>   *Thank you for everything. We'll be back after we have the spear. Please check on my dad and make sure he's safe. We will be careful. I promise.*
>   *—Cassie*

I straightened up the bedspread and placed the note on top of the pillow.

"Ready?" Simone hopped out of the bathroom, putting on her left shoe.

"Yeah." I slung my bag across my body, slipped in the journal, and helped Simone silently push the chair away from the door. I had feared that the old, heavy door would creak as we slowly pulled it open, but it stayed silent. We had managed to make it down the stairs without a sound, but now we faced the three dead bolts on the front door. It didn't matter how careful we were turning each knob, a clanking sound reverberated through the stillness of the monastery as we unlocked each one. I glanced around, but no one showed up.

"Let's go," Simone said, pulling open the door and stepping outside.

I couldn't move. It was like my feet had suddenly been clamped down to the floor. The reality of what I was doing, what I was asking Simone to do, smacked me in the face. I was leaving the supposed security of the monastery and putting everything at risk again. What if I failed or got us both killed? I wasn't really prepared for this kind of thing.

My mouth went dry, and I could barely swallow the lump in my throat.

"What?" Simone looked back at me. "Second thoughts?"

Across the street I could see a chauffeur, wearing his dark suit and driver's cap, standing by a black sedan. We only had to walk over and tell him where we wanted to go.

I took a deep breath. Whether this spear was legit or not, I knew that my choices would determine our destiny, and my dad's.

We'll be fine, I told myself. *We'll find the spear, save my dad, and everything will go back to normal.*

"Seriously, we can go back in." Simone got closer. "I'll stay with you. No matter what, I've got your back."

"No." I took a step forward and closed the door behind me. "We can do this."

We were two steps onto the sidewalk, about to cross the street, when I noticed the chauffeur's profile.

My stomach rolled, and I could feel bile rising to my throat.

His ear . . . the bottom half was missing.

"Simone, stop!" I grabbed her arm. "It's him," I whispered, slowly inching back toward the monastery, trying not to attract attention.

Simone looked up and down the empty street. "Who? No one else is out here."

I was already at the monastery door, trying to open it.

"The guy I saw outside your house. The one I thought looked suspicious right before all the shooting." I shook the door. It didn't budge.

"You sure? I don't . . ."

I ignored her. I glanced back and saw the chauffeur stiffen as our eyes met. He knew I recognized him. I pounded my fist on the monastery door, but there was no time.

"RUN!" I pulled Simone by her shirtsleeve and raced down the street.

"Cassie!" Simone called out, a half step behind me.

"Trust me!" I said, afraid that any minute bullets would fly. We were getting close to an intersection. I didn't dare look back again for fear that the half-eared man was only an arm's length away from grabbing us.

We rounded the corner when a small white car zoomed past us only to slam on the brakes, jump the curb, and block our escape.

The car's passenger door flew open.

"Get in!" Asher shouted.

There was no hesitation. I didn't even stop to consider what Asher was doing driving around at six in the morning or how the half-eared man had come to be our chauffeur. I jumped in, with Simone clambering over me.

"DRIVE!" I yelled.

Asher didn't wait for us to close the door. With Simone sitting on top of me in the front seat, he peeled out, the door slamming shut on its own.

Simone crawled to the back. "I don't see anyone behind us," she said, still catching her breath and looking out the window.

I turned around to confirm we weren't being followed. There was no one.

"Why were you running?" Asher asked, making a quick right onto the larger street of Via Nazionale.

"The chauffeur." I kept looking behind us through the side-view mirror. "He was outside Simone's house when the shooting started. He's one of them."

"Are you sure?" Simone stuck her head between the two seats. "Maybe he just looked like the guy. I mean, I've always used that car service—"

"The guy was missing the bottom half of his ear! It *was* the same guy."

"Fine, fine." Simone inched back. "At least I didn't tell the service where we wanted to go."

Asher didn't slow down, getting us onto the main road of Via Vittorio Veneto and putting as much distance between us and the monastery as possible. Finally catching my breath, I realized that it was too much of a coincidence for Asher to have been driving by when we were being chased.

"Where are you taking us?" I asked him.

"Wherever you want," he answered, stopping behind a garbage truck that was about to turn onto a side street.

"And you just happened to be outside in a car at six in the morning?" Simone questioned him from the backseat. "I don't think you're even old enough to legally drive."

"So? I do a lot of things I'm not old enough to do." He glanced at her through the rearview mirror.

Up ahead I could see a three-story, peach-colored building with a small guardhouse in front. A large American flag was waving from the top of the center balcony. It was the US embassy. I considered how much injury I'd sustain if I jumped out of a moving car.

"Seriously, what were you doing there?" I stared at the building as we passed it. Normally the embassy would be the first place to go for help, but nothing about the last twenty-four hours had been normal. And my father had been very clear about not trusting anyone . . .

Asher took a quick look at me before focusing on the road again. "It was my uncle's idea. He had me waiting outside for you once he saw that you wanted to leave."

"You two were listening to us last night?" Simone asked. "Gross."

"No, *I* don't invade people's privacy," he answered, an obvious reference to our sneaking into his room. "But my laptop has always had remote access. My uncle can see anything you type up."

"Equally creepy," Simone muttered.

"So he was fine with me leaving?" I said, ignoring the back-and-forth between Asher and Simone. It was obvious neither one liked or trusted the other.

"I don't think it's what he wanted, but he knew he couldn't stop you. He was surprised that you'd leave so soon, but since you contacted a driver . . . he knew you were serious and he had to act fast."

It felt like I was a pawn in all this. Where even if I thought decisions were my own, they'd already been calculated by someone else. It didn't matter what choices I made, it felt like my destiny was in someone else's hands.

"Wait, did Brother Gregorio know the half-eared guy would be there?"

"No." Asher kept his eyes on the road. "But he worried someone might come after you. That's why he asked that I follow you. You know, help out if you got into trouble. Guess I was needed a little earlier than expected."

"Yeah, right." Simone shook her head. "He's so worried that he leaves it up to you to protect us."

Protect and serve. That's what Asher had said his job was.

"Zio *is* worried. And he really does want Cassie to be safe." Asher glanced over at me. "You should know that my uncle sacrificed everything when he left his life with the Hastati. He believed that their work protecting the spear was important, but he just couldn't be part of killing innocent people who had the mark. He gave it all up to help people like you."

I nodded, but I could hear Simone grumble something in the back.

My heartbeat finally slowed down to a more normal rhythm as we all fell into an uncomfortable silence. It was strange; even though I barely knew Asher, I did feel safer with him around. Maybe it was a numbers thing. Three people being better than two. Maybe it was something else.

Asher continued driving, making a few turns that led us away from the center of Rome. Finally, he spoke up. "So what's in Civita di Bagnoregio?"

I stayed silent. *How did he know that's where we were going?* Then I remembered that Brother Gregorio could see everything we researched last night.

"That *is* where we're going . . ." Asher paused. "Right?"

Before I could answer, Simone piped up. "We? I don't remember inviting you."

"Your other driver didn't really seem to work out, now did he?" Asher retorted.

I opened my eyes as wide as I could at Simone. She had to be a little nicer to Asher if we wanted his help to get where we needed to go. "It was something my dad mentioned."

"Did he say anything else?"

I realized that if Asher was going to stick with us, I'd have to let him in on what my dad had written. But I wasn't ready to trust him. This was going to be a need-to-know kind of situation. "It's a bit strange, but he said, '*nadie recibe el secreto hasta que el hombre que nadie ve contesta la pregunta,*' which means—"

"No one receives the secret until the man that no one sees answers the question." He grinned, and a dimple appeared high on his cheek. "I took five years of Spanish." He paused for a moment. "So I'm guessing you're going to look for the man no one sees, right?"

"Exactly," I said. "We find him, then hopefully the secret is revealed."

Behind us, Simone was bent over, and I could hear her unzipping something. I turned completely around to see her opening a backpack by her feet. "What's in here, Asher?" she asked, although she was already rummaging through it.

"Just some clothes and stuff I brought along. Didn't know how long I'd be following you."

Simone took inventory. "Water bottles, croissants, a first-aid kit, zip-ties, duct tape . . . a switchblade?"

"For emergencies," he explained matter-of-factly.

"Well, aren't you a Boy Scout," Simone said, then silently mouthed "creepy" to me before taking a bite out of a croissant.

I shrugged, knowing that I wouldn't be able to fully explain why a part of me wanted to trust Asher. It was a gut instinct. Something in the way he looked at me that made me feel like he was on my side. Then again, I *was* supposed to be some kind of oddity that could trigger a change in destiny . . . maybe that's what he was looking at.

"By all means," Asher said, "feel free to have some of my food."

"Thanks," Simone said, her mouth full as she pulled out her phone. "Cassie, can you believe my mom is actually texting me to see how I am?" She pretended to sound annoyed, but I knew better. She secretly craved the attention, even if she would rather die than admit it. "She's already sent me two texts this morning."

"You have a phone? How stupid are you? Get rid of it," Asher commanded.

"No way. I have everything—"

"Simone, he's right. You shouldn't have it on," I said. "They can track us with it."

"If you have to call your mommy," Asher said sarcastically, "you can use one of the burner phones in the side pocket of the bag."

"I don't have to do anything." Simone unzipped the side pocket. "And what's a burner phone?"

"A prepaid cell phone, right?" I had heard the term used in movies when drug dealers or spies wanted to talk to one another. "It can't be traced."

Asher nodded as he turned onto a ramp for the main highway out of Rome. "Yeah, and either throw away your phone or make sure you take the battery out." He glanced at Simone through the rearview mirror. "There are ways the Hastati can trace phones even when they're turned off."

Simone didn't say anything else and instead pulled out her phone battery. She tossed it on the seat next to the bag of croissants and I gave her a quick nod of approval.

I watched as the scenery outside our window changed from cityscape to countryside. Now instead of brick and stucco buildings, we were surrounded by large expanses of dried, grassy fields that lined the autostrada. It reminded me of the weekend road trips my dad would take me on. Just the two of us driving off to explore some new towns like Perugia and Siena: We'd go to the museums or old churches. I wished he were here now.

Suddenly, the warm memory turned cold as I realized that many of those places were written in his notebook. Maybe the trips were part of his search for the spear and had nothing to do with spending time with me. I clenched my teeth. *How could he have kept all this from me? He should've told me. I'd be more prepared to deal with all of it.* Now I was on the run across Italy from unknown assassins and having to figure things out all on my own. *Great job, Papi.*

"Want one?" Simone asked, grabbing another croissant. "Better to eat now than be hungry later."

"Sure," I said, though I really had no appetite.

I took a bite, and in my head I started going over all the things we'd researched the night before.

Asher interrupted my thoughts. "So besides the man that no one sees, what else do you think is in Civita?"

I answered with the truth. "The only thing that seems to matter anymore . . . the spear."

—FOURTEEN—

The four-lane highway sliced through the rolling fields that marked the Italian countryside. Every once in a while I'd see a large villa in the distance or the bell tower of an old church with a small village surrounding it, but mostly it was desolate. Eventually, we left the highway and exited onto a winding road that took us through a wooded area.

We'd been driving for almost two hours and I hadn't even seen a glimpse of Civita di Bagnoregio rising up from the valley like in the pictures. Behind me, Simone had her head leaning against the doorframe. For someone who was so suspicious of Asher, she'd fallen asleep within the first twenty minutes of our trip, leaving me to stare out the window in silence.

"Almost there?" Simone asked, her voice groggy from the nap.

"We're getting close," Asher called back.

We'd just driven by a store selling pottery by the side of the road, which was followed by a bar that had a small restaurant attached. A minute later, more businesses and apartment buildings popped up, with cars, Vespas, and motorcycles lining both sides of the road. A sign indicated that we had just entered Bagnoregio, and before I knew it, we were in the heart of the small town.

But this wasn't Civita di Bagnoregio.

This was the opposite of the Dying City. In Bagnoregio there was life: Residents crossed the streets and made their way to work or school.

The map function on Asher's phone showed that we were still headed in the right direction. As we slowed down in front of the main piazza, I pointed to the cradled phone on the dash. "The footbridge to Civita should be right up ahead. After the church."

"Have you been here before, Asher?" Simone asked, the bumpy cobblestone street making her voice vibrate with each syllable.

"No. I'd never even heard of this place until late last night," Asher said. "Zio woke me up and told me about . . ." He bit the words back, not finishing the last part of his thought.

"Told you what?" I asked.

"Nothing. Just to follow and help you."

Simone scoffed. "Dude, not even Cassie believes that." I shot her a dirty look. "Sorry. You know what I mean," she said to me.

It was obvious that there was more to whatever Brother Gregorio had told Asher. "What did he really tell you?"

Asher shook his head. "He reminded me of my duty."

"Your duty?" I didn't want to be an obligation or someone's charity case. "Well, you don't *have* to do anything. You can drop us off in Civita, and we'll figure things out."

"No, that's not what I meant. I want to be here. Zio has been preparing me for years. I just didn't think I'd have to do it so soon."

"Do what so soon?" I asked.

"This. Deal with the spear. I know how important it is." I could see him looking at me from the corner of his eye. "I know how important *you* are."

I turned and looked out the window. I didn't like the feeling that so much was riding on me. It wasn't fair. Asher might have been training for this for years, but I'd just been told about it.

We were moving at a snail's pace as we squeezed between the buildings of the ever-narrowing street. There were literally only a few inches between the walls and either side of the car. We wouldn't be able to open the doors even if we tried. Then, like squeezing a tube of toothpaste, we were suddenly pushed out onto a road that hugged the side of the mountain. As we rounded the bend, Civita di Bagnoregio came into full view.

It was exactly like the pictures: perched atop a narrow plateau that rose up out of the valley, like a medieval metropolis from the past. The cement footbridge stretched across the valley linking Civita to the town of Bagnoregio and to the present, creating a lifeline for the dying city.

Asher pulled into an empty lot covered in gravel near the entrance of the bridge. We were the only people in the area.

"Let's go," I said, getting out of the car. There was a light wind and the temperature was considerably cooler than in Rome. I immediately zipped up my leather jacket.

Simone pushed up my seat and shrank back once the cold wind entered the car. "With all the cute jackets I have at home . . ." She tugged on the long sleeves of the T-shirt she had borrowed from me before stepping out of the car.

"Here!" Asher was in the back with the trunk open. He tossed a dark-blue sweatshirt at Simone and slung his backpack over his shoulder. "Might not be fashionable, but it's warm and relatively clean."

Simone sniffed it. "Relatively is right," she muttered, but still slipped it on.

I looked up at the crumbling buildings that teetered on the edge of the plateau and the bell tower that sprouted up from the middle of the town. According to our research, in all of Civita there were probably no more than fifteen residents, so I hoped one of them was the man we were looking for . . . even if it was a man who no one saw.

"Before we keep going"—Asher leaned against the car—"we have to go over some ground rules."

"Ground rules?" I turned to face him. "Who put you in charge?" My plan was to get the spear, trade it in for my dad's safety, and have our lives go back to normal. I wasn't about to follow someone else's ideas of what could or could not happen.

"Don't be a control freak, Asher. Cassie is the one with the birthmark, not you." Simone slammed the trunk closed. "We make our own rules."

"Oh, yeah?" Asher dangled the car keys. "Who got you here, and who's taking you back? And who knows more about how the spear really works?" He waited for a moment, then stuffed the keys in his pocket. "Yeah, that would be me. That's why we have to go over some stuff."

I wanted to get going. We were wasting time. "So what are these rules?"

"There's only two of them for now. The first is that, if we get the spear, we all agree to take it back to Brother Gregorio, because he'll know how to get it into the right hands. Okay?"

"That's not really a rule," Simone answered, chewing on one of her fingernails.

"That's fine," I said. "I was planning on doing that anyway. What else?"

"The second one *is* a rule." He looked at Simone, who lifted a single eyebrow in response. "It's that Cassie can never touch the spear. Ever."

"Why?" Simone asked.

"Cassie knows why," Asher answered cryptically.

"It's the binding thing, isn't it?" I asked, recalling the word Brother Gregorio had used the day before and the sentence I had read in the Guardian's Journal.

Asher grimaced, then nodded.

"But it really shouldn't matter if I touch it because the power is stuck inside that bad guy, Tobias, right?" I said. "He's bound to it until he dies."

"Yeah, but he could die at any time. You can't take the chance."

"I don't know," Simone mused. "Would it be so bad if Cassie had that power? I mean, she could choose her own destiny. Pick whatever she wants to happen in the future."

"But I could never choose for things to go back to normal." I looked at Asher for confirmation. "Right?"

He nodded. "And the Hastati would kill you for sure," he added.

"What? Even if I give them the spear?" No one had mentioned being killed if I became bound. Not that I planned on doing that anyway.

"Well, yeah. You need both the bound person and the spear to control destiny. Throughout history whoever was bound to the spear had to be trusted by the Hastati . . . approved by them. I thought you knew that."

I shook my head.

"Oh," Simone said softly.

"Well, I won't be touching it, that's for sure." I stuck my hands in my leather jacket. "Let's just go find it."

As we walked across the footbridge over the gorge between modern Bagnoregio and medieval Civita di Bagnoregio, I kept looking back at the car. It was obvious that there was no one else either behind or ahead of us, and yet I couldn't shake the feeling of being watched.

"Don't worry. I've got an eye out, too," Asher said in a low voice.

I nodded, but wondered exactly who else, besides the half-eared man and the motorcycle-riding assassin, we were supposed to be keeping an eye out for.

As we walked up the steep incline of the bridge, I could hear Simone huffing and puffing next to me. "This is worse than PE," she mumbled.

"It's not too bad." I picked up the pace. The faster we got there the better.

"Please. This is even worse than Latchke's class." She gave me a wink as we finally reached the large stone entrance that had served as Civita's gate centuries earlier.

Walking through the gate's archway, we entered the eerily quiet town. Only the creaking sound of a restaurant sign moving in the wind greeted us. There were no cars, no animals, and no people.

"And the only clue your father gave you was to find the man that no one sees and get him to ask a question?" Asher asked for the third time.

"Yep, that's it," I said.

"The guy might be a hermit . . . that's why no one sees him," Simone speculated. "Especially living in a place like this."

"Guess we'll find out soon enough." I pointed to the restaurant. "Let's ask inside."

Simone followed me, with Asher bringing up the rear, his eyes still scouring the area.

A balding man was behind the restaurant's bar organizing some bottles, his back to us. *"Scusi,"* I said, trying to get his attention from the doorway.

The man turned around and smiled. *"Ah, visitatori!"* He waved us inside. *"Entrare! Entrare!"*

The small restaurant had walls that seemed to have been carved out of the mountain itself, and six small square tables. I couldn't imagine there being many customers, but the town had apparently been "rediscovered" by some travel agents who offered escapes from modern life on weekend day-trips from Rome.

I smiled at the gentleman and leaned closer to Simone. "Ask if he knows of a man that no one sees."

"Ah, American." The man nodded as if he had gained all the information he needed to know about me. "I practice my English," he declared with a strong accent. He walked around the counter and pulled out a bar stool for me. "*Ora dimmi*, how can I help you? You parents around here? You like breakfast?"

Asher spoke in fluent Italian. "No, we're actually in a bit of a hurry and—"

"Tsk, tsk," he chided. "In Civita, there is always time," he said, smiling. "A cappuccino, yes?" He was already walking behind the bar and pulling out three cups and saucers. "I am the owner, Giovanni, and the *caffè* is . . . how you say . . . ?" He turned to pour the milk from a metal pitcher. "Ah, yes." He looked at us over his shoulder. "It is on the house."

The loud whirring sound of the machine steaming the milk drowned out anything else we might say, so we sat on the bar stools and waited. The smell of the espresso brewing made me think of my dad. For as long as I could remember, he always made Cuban coffee first thing in the morning. *"The first drops are the key to making the* espumita *on top. Just like in life, you have to start the right way,"* he'd say as he poured the beginning of the brew into a large mug with sugar in it. The clack, clack, clack noise of the spoon hitting the sides of the cup as he beat the sugar into a creamy froth would jar me awake. *"A good Cuban knows how to make coffee,"* he'd tell me with a smile. Then he'd pour a little of the espresso in a cup of warm milk and let me have a very light version of café con leche.

"Now, you tell me," Giovanni said as he poured the hot milk, followed by a little bit of coffee, into each cup, "what bring you here? You visiting Italy? You are a bit young to be alone."

"No, we are, uh." Asher took a gulp of the coffee to buy some time.

"We're doing research," Simone piped up. "For our school."

"Yes, for a project," I added. "Have you ever heard of a man living in Civita that no one sees?" I asked. "I know this sounds strange."

"No, but this is second time I get asked this." He looked at Asher for clarification. "Maybe it is a man that cannot see? *Un cieco?*"

"No, not a blind man," Asher said. "A man that no one sees. *L'uomo che nessuno si vede,*" he said, translating the riddle to Italian.

Giovanni shrugged.

"You said someone else asked you about this." I tried to gauge his reaction to see if he was really clueless or keeping secrets. "Who was it?"

"A man, I think he said he was a professor in Roma." Giovanni scratched the side of his face. "Is he your teacher? He said he would come back again, because he couldn't find who he was looking for that day."

I wondered if it had been my father. Had he been here and not found the spear?

"Um, yeah. The professor sent us to try and figure it all out. It's a riddle." Simone sipped her coffee. "*Un enigma.* Maybe the man you can't see is someone you normally don't think of."

"Hmm, I don't know." He wiped the bar where a little coffee had splashed. "Like I told your professor the other day, few families live in Civita. Everyone you can see. Everyone see you."

"Well, we should keep asking around anyway." Simone hopped off the bar stool. "Leave something for the coffees, Asher."

"It was on the house," Asher argued, but he was already fishing out a few euros from his pocket.

Outside, the day was getting brighter and warmer, but the town remained vacant. It was easy to see why it was called a dying town. Besides the fact that the buildings were falling into the valley below as the plateau continued to shrink, the people had also left. After thirty minutes of walking around and knocking on different doors, we'd spoken with seven people and none had been able to help. I was starting to think that this was a waste of time. That I'd misinterpreted what my dad wrote. Maybe he'd already come here and found nothing. Maybe the dying city was Detroit and CDB was someone's initials.

But even if I was wrong about this place, I couldn't give up until I was absolutely sure. "Up there." I pointed to a second-floor window. "I think I saw someone."

Asher ran—no, it was more like he flew up the steps. One foot barely touched every fourth step before he was up in the air again. In the blink of an eye he was at the top, grinning down at me. He turned and knocked on the door.

"Did you see what he just did?" I asked.

Simone sat down on the first step and shrugged. "So he's fast and knows a little parkour. Big deal." She took off her shoes and stretched out her toes. "Why don't you go up with him? I'll wait here and give my feet a break."

"Want to switch?" I offered, lifting up my brown flats.

"No." She slipped her feet back into her shoes. "I think wearing your size sixes on a size-eight foot would be worse. I'll buy some shoes later." Simone pulled out the burner phone from her pocket. "My mom just texted me. She says she's flying back to Rome."

"I thought you'd taken out the battery from that phone after you replied to her earlier text. You know that's the whole point of these burner phones. One use and done."

Simone smiled. "You've watched too many spy movies, Cassie. I doubt someone figured out that I was the one texting her when she gets a million texts every day. Plus, my mom has more security and antihacking systems than most governments. It'll be fine. I'll just send her a quick reply." She started typing.

I stared at her, not saying a word. This didn't seem like a good idea.

"What?" Simone paused and looked at me. "Listen, I'll pull out the battery afterward just in case. I just want to send this one text. This parent-being-worried thing, it's something new for me."

Asher's voice from the top of the stairs caught our attention, and we both looked up. He was speaking with someone.

"Go keep an eye on Parkour Boy and I'll wait for you here," Simone said.

There was no time to waste. "Okay," I said, hurrying up the steps. "I'll be right back."

"Who else is there?" asked the old woman, in Italian, as I approached. She was staring straight ahead, but there was a cloudy glaze covering each eyeball that created an unnatural tint of blue. Behind her, the house was completely dark.

"Mi chiamo Cassie," I said, realizing she was blind.

"Eh?" She leaned forward, her arm outstretched.

I took her crinkly hand in mine and repeated. "Cassie. Cassandra."

She touched my ring and nodded. "Ah, Cassandra." The old woman then touched her chest and said, *"Io sono Signora Pescatori."*

"Nice to meet you, Signora Pescatori," I answered in my best Italian.

"She told me she's the oldest person in Civita and that she's never heard of a man that no one sees," Asher said.

My shoulders dropped. It wasn't completely unexpected, but I was still holding out hope that someone knew what my father was talking about. We were running out of options.

"Grazie, signora. Arrivederci." I turned to go down the steps.

"No!" The old woman stumbled out of the doorway into Asher's arms. She put up her hands and felt his face with her fingertips. She asked him something in Italian, her voice quivering just a bit.

"Where am I?" Asher chuckled. "I'm right here, on your doorstep. You're not going to fall."

"No." She shook her head defiantly. *"Dimmi dove,"* she repeated, an expectant tone in her voice.

Asher looked down at the floor, and then over at me. "I'm here in front of your door."

Signora Pescatori looked confused by his answer. "No." She waited a moment, then pushed away from Asher as hard as she could. "No, no, no!" she yelled and threw her hands up in the air, muttering something else under her breath.

We stood there in shock at her sudden change in mood.

"Vai via," she said, shooing us away. "Go away!" she yelled again in Italian as she slammed the door.

"That is one crazy lady," Asher noted as we walked down the stairs.

"What was that all about?" Simone asked. "Asher trying to make more friends?"

"Very funny," he answered. "I don't see you trying to figure any of this out."

I walked away from the two of them toward the railing that overlooked the valley and the barren hills that stretched out as far as the eye could see. This was the current edge of Civita, but it wouldn't be long before more of the mountain would crumble and fall into the valley below, continuing Civita's demise. Just down the street, the only thing that remained of the old palace was its front facade, the back walls and rooms having already dropped the three hundred plus feet to the valley floor below. It was a reminder that even in Civita, time would take its toll. And time was something I didn't have much of.

I kicked a small rock over the edge of the cliff a few feet in front of me and twisted the Hastati ring around my finger. If I didn't figure this out, I'd have to go back to the monastery and wait for another clue or for someone else to find the spear.

"Think, Cassie. Think!" I pounded my head with my fist.

"Maybe we're going about this the wrong way," Asher said, coming up to stand next to me.

Simone leaned against the railing on my other side. "Maybe we're going about this the wrong way," she repeated in a voice almost identical to Asher's.

"I don't sound like that," Asher said dryly, but a part of him had to be impressed with her talent.

"You actually do, but whatever," Simone retorted. "So tell us, O Wise One, what should we be doing?"

"*You* can be quiet. And, Cassie"—his expression softened when he looked at me—"I want you to close your eyes and think back to what your father told you." Asher waited for me to do this, and when I didn't, he continued. "There could be a clue in how or what he said."

I bit my lip. The journal was in the small messenger bag right next to my hip, but I hadn't wanted to show it to him. "Um, well, he didn't so much as say it. He more or less . . ."

Asher's eyebrows scrunched together, forming a little vertical line between them. "Wait, didn't you say he told you to come to Civita and the thing about the man no one sees? Did you make that up?"

"No, of course not. He really did tell me." I was feeling uneasy with all the questions. "It's just I don't know if I should say exactly . . ."

"Hold on." Asher took a step back. "If you're not telling me everything, how am I supposed to help?"

"No one here asked for your help," Simone chimed in.

"I know, but Cassie agreed in the car to—"

"Whoa, whoa, whoa. I didn't agree to anything except letting you come with us," I said. Asher might seem trustworthy, but I was not about to drop my guard.

"Yeah, but you already told me about the riddle," Asher argued. "So if I'm helping find this mystery man, I need to know all the facts."

"He has a point," Simone interjected.

"What?" I couldn't believe that Simone, of all people, was siding with Asher.

Simone continued. "I mean, what difference will it make if he knows your dad wrote you the message as opposed to telling you? Maybe those years in the monastery could come in handy. Don't monks rewrite the Bible and stuff for fun?"

I glared at her. It wasn't Simone's job to spill my secrets.

"What?" She widened her eyes. "You know I'm right. It's for the best."

"So wait, your dad wrote it down somewhere?" Asher's eyes danced with excitement. "You know, if it's a code that your dad created, I might be able to crack it. First letter of each word might spell out something. Maybe it's a rotational pattern. I don't know. The Hastati use a lot of codes, so I've had some training in deciphering them."

"My dad isn't Hastati." I grasped the top of my messenger bag. "At least I don't think so."

I didn't know what to do. Simone shouldn't have said anything. Sharing all the information I had with Asher wasn't part of my original plan, but he did know a lot more than we did about the Hastati, the spear, and codes. Maybe Simone was right.

Asher gazed down at me. "Cassie?" he asked. "Are you going to show me?"

I went through all the pros and cons in my head. It boiled down to the fact that Asher had helped us, and yet, there was still something that felt off. It was in his eyes. He was keeping a secret, but I couldn't tell if it was about me or not.

"I didn't find anything hidden in here." I opened up the bag and pulled out the notebook. "But you might be able to find a clue."

Asher looked surprised. "Is that the Guardian's Journal?"

"No, we really did leave that one behind," I explained as Asher flipped through the pages. "This is more of a personal notebook that my dad kept."

Simone pulled the sweatshirt off and tied it around her waist. "But it did have the stuff about the dying city, so maybe there's something else in it."

Asher crouched down and flipped through the pages. "Your dad made a lot of sketches of things. There are even a few of you." He stopped to analyze the drawing, and then looked up at me. "He's actually pretty good."

"I know," I said. "His whole life is about art. It's how he sees things."

"Hm." Asher stared at the last sentence for a couple of minutes. "If it's a code, it isn't a basic one. I've studied medieval codes, Renaissance cryptanalysis, and ciphers of the Dark Ages, and this doesn't seem to fit any of the ones I remember."

Simone shook her head. "Such a freak," she said under her breath just as a loud "*Buongiorno* again!" rang out.

The restaurant owner, Giovanni, had just stepped out from a side door in a nearby building. A little girl, no more than four or five years old, trailed after him. "Did you find the man you are looking for?" he asked, carrying a crate full of potatoes.

"No," I answered. "Still searching."

Giovanni stopped, and the little girl hid behind his legs, trying to peek around to see us. "Try upstairs." Giovanni lifted his chin and motioned up to the crazy old woman's apartment. "Signora Pescatori is older than these mountains. She knows more than anyone."

The little girl stuck her head a little farther out and smiled. Asher gave her a small wave, causing her to dart back behind Giovanni.

"We already asked her," Simone responded. "She didn't know."

"Oof, if Nonna Nadie does not know . . ." He pursed his lips as if in pain. "Too bad, but if you are hungry later, you come by the restaurant. I am making gnocchi. Better to think on a full stomach, no?"

"Nonna Nadie?" I asked.

"Signora Pescatori. We call her Nonna because she is like the town's grandmother."

Giovanni was still saying something, but I'd stopped listening. All I could think of was that Signora Pescatori's first name was Nadie.

I stared off into space and thought about the note written in my father's journal. *En la ciudad que se está muriendo, nadie recibe el secreto hasta que el hombre que nadie ve contesta la pregunta.* Could it be a play on words? I had translated the Spanish word *nadie* both times to its most common meaning of "no one," but what if it actually referred to a woman's name . . . Nadie. So it would actually say "in the city that is dying, no one receives the secret until the man that Nadie sees answers the question." The old woman had the secret!

"Hey, Cassie," Simone called out. "You okay?"

Asher snapped his fingers in front of my face, his ring flashing before my eyes. "Cassie?"

"Huh, what?" I blinked and looked around. Giovanni and the little girl were already gone. "Oh, yeah. I'm fine." I started chuckling, which turned into a full-on laugh attack. All my worry had finally found its release in the form of hysterical laughter.

"Cassie, you're not acting normal." Simone got closer to me and touched my forehead as if I had a fever. "What's going on?"

"Oh, oh." I bent over and caught my breath. "You're not going to believe it." Asher was now next to Simone, giving me an equally concerned look. "Brace yourself . . . I think I figured out who we're looking for."

"You did? Who's the man that no one sees?" Simone asked.

I smiled from ear to ear and pointed to Asher. "He is! And he's going to get the secret for us!"

—FIFTEEN—

"Cassie, come on." Simone cocked her head to the side. "He can't be the man that no one sees. He's not even a real man."

"Excuse me?" Asher raised his voice.

Simone waved off his comment. "You know what I mean. You're, what . . . sixteen? Seventeen?"

"Fifteen," he replied dryly.

"Only fifteen? Wow. Okay, well, that makes my point even more." Simone continued, "Your father was definitely not talking about a fifteen-year-old boy being the key to this thing. Plus, we can all see him."

"You don't get it." I took the notebook from Asher. "Look at what my father wrote." I pointed to the words. "In Spanish *nadie* means 'no one,' which is why we kept translating it to *nessuno* in Italian for everyone here, but I think the second *nadie* refers to the name Nadie, with a capital *N*." I let the idea sink in. "That's Signora Pescatori's first name."

"But she's blind, she doesn't—" Asher stopped in mid-sentence and nodded in agreement.

"What? I don't get it," Simone complained, looking back and forth between Asher and me.

"She can see with her hands," I explained. "When she grabbed me or touched Asher's face. That's how Nadie sees. We have to talk to her again. Have Asher be the person she sees, have him answer her question, and maybe she'll tell us where the spear is."

Asher's shoulders slumped. "Problem is, she didn't really ask us anything besides who we were. She threw us out, remember?"

"Maybe you didn't say it the right way." Simone had a glimmer in her eye. "You might have forgotten something."

"Oh, please, enlighten us. How would you suggest we do it?" Asher crossed his arms in front of his chest. "And don't say that it's by using the magic words like *please* or *thank you*."

"Nope." She pointed to his pocket. "Magic comes from the sound of euro bills rubbing together." Simone paused. "Cold hard cash will get her to open up. It always works."

"That's stupid," Asher answered with disgust. "You can't just buy people's help."

"Sorry, Simone, but I think he's right," I added gently. "She's not the type. There has to be something we're missing."

"Pfft." Simone pursed her lips. "Everyone has a price . . . even if they don't know it."

"Maybe she wanted our full names," Asher said. "We only told her our first names."

"Or she needs to know about being a Guardian or that I'm marked. Maybe she can only tell her secret to someone like us. It might even be that she has the spear!" Suddenly, I was excited. This felt like a real possibility.

"But what if you're wrong? We shouldn't be telling people—"

"This has to be it!" Simone grabbed my hand and pulled me toward the apartment. "Let's go!"

Simone and I ran as fast as we could, but Asher quickly passed us, hurdling over a couple of potted plants and scaling the half wall that divided one building's patio area from another's before sprinting up the steps. By the time I got there, he was already looking through a small window. I knocked on the door, but there was no answer.

"Signora Pescatori?" I waited. "Signora Pescatori!"

Nothing.

"You think she left?" Simone asked.

"No, I see her sitting in a chair in there," Asher said. "She's ignoring us. *Signora*, we're here to answer your question!" he said loudly in Italian as he rapped on the window.

"There's a Guardian here!" Simone shouted at the old woman.

"SHHH!" Asher jumped in front of Simone. "Do you not know the meaning of secrecy?"

Simone shrugged.

Asher turned and leaned against the wall. "We're missing something. She wasn't angry with us at first. What did we do to get her so upset?"

"I don't know. She was fine when we told her our names."

Asher nodded in agreement. "It was when we were about to leave that she reached out and touched my face—that's when she got all crazy."

"Well, that could upset anybody," Simone declared with a grin.

I gave her a disapproving look. Now was not the time for snide remarks.

"Maybe the answer is in your dad's book." I passed it to him, and he flipped through the pages. "Or think back, maybe he told you something about it and you just forgot . . ."

"My dad didn't go around teaching me how to answer cryptic questions from old Italian women. I think I'd remember that. Plus, all she kept asking was 'Where are you?' And there's no other way to answer that except the way you did."

"Actually." Asher paused his search through the book and looked up at me. "She didn't say that. She asked where was I standing."

"That doesn't make sense," Simone said. "Weren't you standing in front of her?"

Where are you standing? The question triggered a memory of my dad. Papi had always loved to use art to talk to me about life. His favorite was *"You are the artist of your own life—what colors do you want to use?"* but I now remembered him asking me when I was little, *"Where are you standing in the painting—in the light or in the shadow?"* I'd purposely say in the shadow, so he'd chase and tickle me until I gave up and said the answer he wanted: *"I stand in the light."*

Could that have been his way of teaching me to say the right answer?

"I think my dad did tell me," I muttered. "We needed to say 'I stand in the light.'"

"You sure?" Asher didn't seem convinced. "That sounds a bit strange."

"If Cassie says it"—Simone gave me an approving nod—
"then that's what it is." She waved her hands, pointing to
everything around us. "And seriously, what about all of this
hasn't been strange?"

"Signora!" I yelled through the window, but the old
woman was no longer in her chair. "I stand in the light!"

Nothing.

"Mi trovo nella luce!" Asher repeated in Italian.

Before we could say anything else there was a click of the
door. Signora Pescatori stood there . . . a big, toothless smile
on her face.

"Finalmente!" The old woman stretched out her hands,
her fingers touching Simone's face and hair. "No!" She
recoiled and pushed Simone away as if she had just touched
something vile. "No, no, no!" she repeated, swatting her
away. "Where is *he*?" she asked in heavily accented English.
"The one who stands in the light."

"You speak English?" Simone asked, a surprised look on
her face.

Before Signora Pescatori could answer, Asher rushed over,
stuffed my dad's notebook in his jacket, and took her wrinkled hands in his own. "I'm the one who answered the
question. Asher . . . from a little while ago."

"Yes, yes. I had hoped you would come back." She hugged
him tightly. "I can see that you are handsome and brave. A
true protector."

"Ha!" Simone made a face. "She really is blind."

Asher glared at Simone before turning his attention back

125

to the old woman. "Signora Pescatori, do you have the spear?"

Signora Pescatori gave him one more squeeze and whispered something in his ear. Then she began feeling his hands.

"She said she has something to give us, but that she first needs to read our palms," Asher explained. He looked at Simone. "Even yours."

"Of course she does, because this hasn't been weird enough," Simone muttered.

Signora Pescatori finished analyzing Asher's hand and reached over to touch his chest. She spoke slowly enough that I could understand most of what she said. "Stay true and trust your heart. Don't listen to what others tell you, for the wrong decision will haunt you."

Asher glanced at me for a moment before nodding.

"Here." Simone thrust her palm into Signora Pescatori's hands. "Let's get this over with."

The old woman stroked the center of Simone's palm, concentrating on every line and curve. She didn't say anything while doing this, but would occasionally shake her head and sigh. Finally, when she was done, she grabbed Simone's wrist and lowered her voice to just above a whisper. "You are not as strong as you pretend, and submission will be your undoing. If you remain weak, you will lose what is most important."

Simone pulled her hand back. "I never submit . . . to anyone." She turned and faced me. "You can listen to this stupid stuff if you want, but I won't."

"Simone . . ." I pleaded. She couldn't just leave when we were so close to possibly getting the spear.

"Uh-uh. No way. This lady is crazy. Calling *me* weak?" She stormed down the stairs.

"Where are you going?" I called out.

She stopped on the last step. "I don't know." Then, a split second later, she corrected herself. "Actually, I do know. I'll meet you at the restaurant. I'm going to see if Giovanni has any more information."

"You can't wait a few more minutes until we're done?" Asher asked.

Simone narrowed her eyes and looked up at Signora Pescatori. "No." Then she took off down the street.

A tension hung in the air. We couldn't afford to have Signora Pescatori shut us out again if she had the spear, but I hated having Simone go off by herself. I had to get us back on track.

"Read mine," I said, giving her my hand. "Tell me what you see."

Signora Pescatori traced the lines of my palm, then touched every bit of skin up to my fingertips. She again said nothing, but when she was done she reached up and put both hands around my face. "Difficult choices to be made by someone so young." She looked pained. "Each choice we make determines destiny, so think wisely before choosing. The time is close at hand."

It was those same words the gypsy had said in the subway

station. Choices and destiny. It was like the idea was haunting me.

Signora Pescatori took a step back into her dark apartment. She felt her way around a chair and then to a small desk. I could see her opening a drawer and pulling something out.

"Do you think she's getting the spear?" Asher whispered.

I shrugged as the old woman came back to the door carrying something wrapped in blue velvet. I held my breath as she slipped off the cloth to reveal a wooden box. It was intricately carved with a leaf pattern all around except for a circle on the top that resembled a pinwheel, where each wedge was a different shade of red. "I've been waiting many years to give this to someone. And you will both play a part in what is coming." She ran her fingers over the leaves and the smoothness of the circle. She held it out for us to take.

"*Grazie*," I said, reaching for the box.

"No." Asher took it from her hands. "I'll hold it."

Signora Pescatori reached over and touched the side of my face. "Such beauty," she said wistfully. "I was once young like you." She took a step back into her apartment. "Very important that you know that the key is in the eye of the beholder."

"All right, but what did you mean about both of us playing a part in something?" I asked.

"I have fulfilled my duty," the old woman said with a content look on her face. "Just remember that it is important

128

to . . ." She lifted her nose and sniffed the air. Her expression changed, and her blue-glazed eyes narrowed. "You must go . . . quickly."

"Why? What's happening?" Asher turned to look past the stone building and over to the piazza. I followed his gaze and saw the same desolate scene from the morning. The empty, dusty street led to the piazza, where the only sign of life was the open door of Giovanni's restaurant. Looking in the other direction, there was only the railing that ran alongside the crumbling cliff about fifty yards away.

"You must open the box when you can no longer see," Signora Pescatori said quickly, then grabbed the edge of the door. "And now you must hurry and leave."

I stuck my foot in the doorway, not letting her close it on us. "Why? And what do you mean when we can't see?"

"Go! Get out!" She kicked my leg away and slammed the door in my face.

I stood still, dumbfounded at having the door slammed on me for a second time by the old woman. She had once again gone from strange to absolutely nuts in the blink of an eye.

"Let's get out of here." Asher nudged me, carrying the box down the stairs like he was balancing glasses filled with water, making sure its contents weren't jostled or shaken.

"It's in there, right?" I asked, following him down the steps. The intricately designed box had to house the ancient spear.

"I can't tell." Asher gently moved the box up and down, testing its weight. "It might be cushioned against something. We'll have to open it and see."

"Hold on. I want to get Simone."

"Why? She took off. She doesn't deserve to see us open it." Asher pointed to a narrow alley between two stone buildings. "Let's just go over there in case someone is watching."

"No, we're a team. We open it together." I pulled him by his sleeve and headed toward Giovanni's restaurant. "Come on."

It was obvious the moment we stepped into the restaurant that no one was there. It was eerily quiet. Immediately, I regretted letting Simone go off by herself. Something was definitely off. Even for a place like Civita di Bagnoregio.

"Simone?" Asher called out, but there was no answer. "Giovanni?"

I stepped back outside and scanned the area. Signora Pescatori was nervous about something. Maybe we weren't safe standing around.

Asher walked up behind me. "No one's in there."

I had the strangest sensation of wanting to run. It was like every instinct was telling me to hurry up and get out. "We need to find Simone and go."

"Agreed." Asher checked around the corner of the building. "But we can't attract attention. Something doesn't feel right."

I was relieved to know that it wasn't only me being paranoid. "She's probably around here looking for Giovanni. Maybe where we saw him last time carrying the potatoes."

He put the wooden box in his backpack. "Let's check there."

We hurried up the street, staying close to the buildings and in the shadows. "I really hope she isn't stupid enough to go too far or get lost," Asher whispered as we approached an alley.

"She isn't," I said, trailing a couple of steps behind him. "Simone's one of the smartest people I know. She's not only book-smart, but street-smart."

"What does a spoiled rich girl know about the street? Chances are—"

Asher didn't finish his sentence; instead, he whirled around and pushed me away from the corner and back against the building. "Shh." He raised a finger to his lips.

I could feel his heart beating against my chest. "What is it?" I could barely get the words out.

"The half-eared man is here," Asher whispered. "He has Simone."

—SIXTEEN—

Survival instincts sometimes come down to a simple choice: fight or flight. In this case there was only one choice . . . fight. Leaving Simone was not an option.

"We have to get her." I pushed Asher away and took a step forward.

"No." He pulled me back. "They won't hurt her. The one the Hastati want is you."

"I don't care. If you don't want to save her, that's fine, but I'm not letting them take her."

"You can't just rush over there. That won't help anyone." He looked up and down the street. "Don't move." He crept along the wall until he could take a quick peek around the corner.

I followed him so when he stepped back he bumped into me. He scowled, but I didn't care. I wasn't about to sit around and do nothing while my best friend was in danger.

"He has her cornered at the end of a dead-end street," Asher muttered.

"Uh-huh. So what do we do?"

He looked up at the building next to us. I could tell he was coming up with a plan.

"Okay. I think I can get up on the roof of this place, but you have to do exactly what I tell you." He took off his back-pack and put it on the ground.

"Go on." I wasn't going to make any promises until I heard his plan.

"I'm going to go up there and jump down on the guy while—"

"You're *what*?"

"Listen, I know how to make jumps like that. I'm going to knock him down, but you have to be ready to run." He pointed across the main piazza. "If Simone and I don't catch up, you have to leave and get back to the monastery. Take the backpack with you, but don't open the box. Understand?"

This was a repeat of what had happened with my dad. Except this time I wasn't going to do what I was told. "Got it," I answered, knowing it was a lie. I wouldn't abandon Simone.

I tried to calm myself down while Asher disappeared around the other side of the building. The more I thought about his plan, the more worried I got. I needed to find a weapon of some sort so I could help. I tried picking up one of the nearby potted plants, but they were too heavy. *If only I could find something.*

"Psst."

I looked up to see Asher on the edge of the roof. He pointed back toward the restaurant and mouthed "Run that way."

That's when I saw his right hand. He had a wooden stick, a broom handle, in it. He wasn't completely unprepared. Maybe this would work. Besides, there wasn't much else we could do.

I nodded.

He disappeared, and I peered around the corner for the first time. Simone was sitting on the ground, but she was talking to the half-eared guy. Was she trying to buy her way out? That would be typical Simone. But it might be working, because whatever she was saying, she definitely had his attention.

That was when Asher jumped.

It was like straight out of the movies. He came flying down, landed right on the half-eared guy, knocked him to the ground, then rolled away from him.

As Asher tumbled, the impact of the fall forced the broom handle out of his hand. It bounced and clattered against the cobblestones.

"Run!" Asher yelled as the half-eared guy started to get up.

Simone didn't waste a moment. She ran down the street toward me as Asher tackled the half-eared guy.

"Cassie!" Simone screamed. I shoved the backpack into her hands and ran past her toward Asher. Bending down, I scooped up the broom handle and, just as the half-eared man pinned Asher to the ground, I swung and hit the man squarely on the side of the head.

The half-eared man collapsed on top of Asher. Blood trickled out of a gash on the side of his head, but it looked like he was still breathing.

"What are you doing?" Asher exclaimed, pushing the half-eared man off him. "You were supposed to run!"

"You're welcome," I said, tossing the stick off to the side and hiding the fact that my hands were shaking.

"Yeah, well, thanks." Asher glanced down at the unconscious man. "But we have to get out of here."

"I know."

We both ran toward the end of the alley where Simone was standing, holding the backpack in her hands.

"Is he dead?" Simone had a horrified look on her face.

"No, and he'll probably wake up any minute," Asher answered, taking the backpack from her and swinging it over his shoulder. "Now let's go."

I took two steps and noticed Simone wasn't coming. She was frozen in place staring at the half-eared man, who had started to stir.

"Simone!" I pulled her by the arm, but that wasn't what snapped her out of her trancelike state. It was the rumbling sound that reverberated through the stillness of the town.

We both looked at each other, our eyes wide with fear. There was no mistaking the noise. It was a motorcycle.

Had the motorcycle-riding assassin found us, too? Were they working together?

Asher turned to face us. "Not good," he said.

He was right. Our time was up.

—SEVENTEEN—

We had to get back to the car, and we had to do it fast.

"Over there!" Asher pointed to Giovanni's restaurant, where two bicycles and a Vespa were leaning against a wall. "One of you can ride on the handle bars while I pedal."

I gave him a small nod and we all ran across the piazza toward them.

Just as we were about to reach the bikes someone yelled, *"Americani!"* It was Giovanni. He was calling to us from the steps of the nearby church. "A man," he said. "He is looking for you!"

I raised a finger to my lips, hoping he would be quiet. We were trying to avoid any attention.

"He say he has something for you!" Giovanni kept shouting. He didn't understand that, whoever it was, what they had for me was a bullet with my name on it. "He might help you find the man that no one sees."

"Change of plans!" Asher pushed the bikes off the Vespa. "The key's in the ignition!" He hopped on the scooter and turned the key.

Simone quickly pushed aside a large bag of coffee beans and climbed into the Vespa's sidecar.

"Che! What you doing?" Giovanni's demeanor quickly changed. "No, no! That is mine!"

Giovanni was now running toward us from across the square. I jumped on the seat behind Asher, wrapping my arms around his chest, the backpack in my face.

"We're only borrowing it!" I said as Asher hit the gas.

Giovanni chased after us, but we quickly left him behind, huffing and puffing.

The uneven cobblestones and Simone's weight made the Vespa wobble wildly from side to side. We had made a quick right turn through a small courtyard and were now exiting onto a different side street. I kept my eyes peeled for the half-eared guy or someone on a motorcycle, but saw no one. For all we knew, the motorcycle we'd heard might have nothing to do with us, but we couldn't take the chance. Plus, the half-eared guy was there, and he was bound to wake up soon.

Once at the footbridge, we zoomed across to the gravel parking lot, then pulled up next to our car. The three of us jumped out, the ground crackling and crunching beneath our feet.

"NO!" Asher exclaimed, staring at the car's slashed tires.

I ran to the other side. All four tires were cut.

"Get back on the Vespa!" Simone yelled. "There's a motorcycle on the bridge!"

I jerked my head and confirmed what Simone was seeing. From where we stood, I couldn't see if his helmet had the red flames, but it didn't matter. This wasn't a coincidence and we had no time to spare.

We jumped back on the Vespa and sped up the road to the main part of town. We managed to lose him by making a few sharp turns, but he was only a short distance behind us. We weren't going to outrun him on the scooter. We had to figure out another way to escape.

"Look over there!" I pointed to a blue regional Cotral bus that was dropping off some passengers.

Asher slammed on the brakes. "Go! Make sure it doesn't leave. I'll hide this thing so he doesn't know where we went."

Simone and I jumped out. The sign on the top of the bus said Orvieto. I didn't know where that was, but I didn't care. The farther away we got from the Hastati, the better. Two women, who by the looks of their cropped pants, polar fleece jackets, and big cameras had to be tourists, were already boarding the bus. They each had their bus tickets out, but the driver didn't bother to look up from his newspaper as they took two window seats near the front.

Simone pushed me from behind. "Just get on," she whispered. We both knew that tickets weren't sold on buses, but we had gotten a lucky break . . . the driver didn't seem to care whether we had them or if they were validated. We got on the bus, walked past the two women and a handful of other passengers, and headed toward the very back.

I looked out the window for Asher. There was a young woman pushing a baby stroller down the sidewalk and a police officer standing at the opposite corner next to a shoe store. Cars were passing by, but the morning activity had died down considerably. Up front, the bus driver stretched, folded his newspaper, and checked his watch. "Isn't Asher coming?" I asked Simone.

The bus began to rumble, and I could feel the gears shifting.

Asher had to hurry. I pressed my face against the glass to see farther down the street. There was some movement in the distance. Someone was running toward us, but we had already started to roll forward, the driver braking only to merge into traffic.

"*Un momento!*" I shouted, pushing past Simone's legs and rushing up the aisle. "Please!" I pointed out the front window where Asher was waving trying to get the driver's attention.

The driver glanced back at me through the rearview mirror, then looked ahead to where I was pointing. He sighed and opened the door just as Asher got there.

"*Grazie,*" Asher mumbled, a bit out of breath, as he climbed aboard.

"*Biglietto?*" The driver expected Asher to show his validated ticket.

Asher shook the driver's hand instead and once again said, "*Grazie.*"

The driver briefly looked at his hand, where Asher had slipped him a fifty-euro bill, then motioned for Asher to move along. Asher gave me a look and shrugged. It was something Simone would've done.

"What took you so long?" I asked as Asher got close and the bus began its merge onto the main road.

Asher carefully took off his backpack and placed it on an

empty seat next to him. "I couldn't leave the Vespa nearby. It'd draw too much attention."

The bus lurched forward, but I stayed standing, keeping my balance by holding onto one of the seatbacks.

"Get down!" Asher grabbed my arm and pulled me next to him. "You too, Simone." His eyes were fixed on something outside. "Get down!"

Miraculously, Simone did as he said without even asking a question.

I stayed crouched down, sharing the seat with Asher, but peered out through the bottom of the window. A slow-moving motorcycle was coming toward us, the driver holding up traffic as he scoured the area. It was the man with the curly hair who had shot my dad and showed up at the hospital afterward. He was wearing jeans instead of all black and wasn't wearing the helmet, but I was certain it was him.

"That's the guy that shot my dad," I whispered, ducking my head again.

"He's Hastati," Asher said, his breath hitting the side of my ear. "I saw him once at the monastery. Zio met him at the door. Wouldn't even let him in."

The bus and the motorcycle passed each other, and we continued in the opposite direction from where the motorcyclist was heading. It seemed like we had gotten away.

After a minute or two, we all heaved a collective sigh and eased back up in our seats.

"See, that's why I wanted to hide the Vespa. Now he won't have any idea where we went."

I crawled away from him and went back across the aisle to my seat next to Simone. "Yeah, but you almost missed the bus."

"I would've caught up to you." I could see him finally relaxing. "Cassie, I'm in this all the way with you. You have to know that by now."

And I did know it. But I also knew that I couldn't completely let my guard down with someone I'd just met.

"Now that we're all together, let's open the box," I said.

"Here?" Asher lowered his voice to barely a whisper. "Are you crazy?"

I looked at the few people sitting toward the front of the bus. "No one is watching. It's private enough."

"Wait." Simone grabbed my arm. "Did that crazy old lady actually have the spear?"

Asher unzipped his backpack and pulled out the box. "You'd know if you hadn't taken off and gotten yourself caught."

"Hey! I didn't ask to be grabbed, you know. And I could've handled it myself."

"Whatever." Asher stared at the clasp on the box. "I think you have to unscrew this to get it to open."

I realized that we hadn't had a chance to talk to Simone about what had happened to her. "He didn't hurt you, did he?"

Simone shook her head and I gave her a hug.

"Did he say anything to you?" I asked. "I saw you talking before Asher jumped him."

She pulled away. "Not really. He wanted to know where you were. If we'd found out anything." Simone glanced out the window at a car passing by. "I didn't tell him anything."

"Well, I'm just glad we got you away from him," I said, giving her arm a gentle squeeze. "I can't do this without my sidekick."

Simone gave me a weak smile and pointed to the box. "So, is the spear inside?"

"We don't know," I replied as Asher fumbled with the clasp.

"Got it," he said victoriously. He looked up at me. "Ready?"

"Wait. Signora Pescatori said to be sure we opened it when we couldn't see. Maybe we should close our eyes while you lift the lid."

"Of course there would be something weird to opening the box," Simone muttered.

Asher shot Simone a look. "Good idea, Cassie. We'll all close our eyes, and on the count of three I'll lift the top."

I squeezed my eyes shut.

"Are your eyes closed?" he asked.

"Yes," we both answered.

I heard Asher flip open the clasp. I held my breath. This was it.

"Three . . . two . . . I'm lifting the top . . . now."

I opened my eyes, half-expecting there to be rays of light streaming out from inside the box. At the very least I expected to see an old metal spearhead about the size of my hand, like the one Brother Gregorio had shown me in the book.

Simone gasped.

"It can't be!" Asher flipped the box over, not wanting to believe what we could all see.

Or better said . . . what we couldn't see.

The box was empty!

EIGHTEEN

"Why am I not surprised?" Simone said.

"No, it can't be." I grabbed the empty box from Asher and shook it. *All this work for nothing?* Tears stung my eyes. I wasn't sad; I was angry. There was no way it could all end like this. We were too close. There had to be more.

Simone put a hand on my shoulder. "Maybe she made a mistake. Gave you the wrong box. We can go back there another day."

"No, she knew what she was doing. It's the right box," Asher mumbled.

Simone rolled her eyes. "For heaven's sake, she's an old, crazy, blind woman." Simone's voice was strained. "Emphasis on BLIND!"

"Simone, you didn't see her." I ran my fingers over each groove of the box. "Signora Pescatori felt the carvings along the edge of the box before giving it to us . . . she knew what she was doing. She even gave us instructions about opening it when we couldn't see." I flipped the box and shook it once more. "It must mean something."

"Fine, maybe it does." Simone relented. "But then we should call someone and see if they know about the box. I can ask—"

"Of course!" Asher interrupted. "We can ask Zio. He'll probably know what it is." Asher took out one of the burner phones.

"Hold on." I reached over to stop Asher. "Won't someone be listening or tracing the call?"

"No, it should be fine. At least for about a minute. We have a state-of-the-art scrambler and a rerouting network that should buy us some time," Asher explained. "It has to do with a cell phone always communicating with the closest cell tower that—"

"Whatever." Simone cut him off. "How about I use one of those untraceable phones to search the Internet. Odds are I'll find something before you do." She held out her hand.

Asher hesitated, but then handed her a new phone.

"You sure they can't trace the call if it's less than a minute?" I didn't want to take a chance at being caught on the bus.

"I'm sure. It should take the very best hacker at least a minute."

"Okay, so call and talk fast," I said. "We'll time you."

"It'll still mean we use up another phone. Then we'll only have the one Simone has and the one left in the bag."

"We need answers, so it's not like we have a choice," I said. "Simone, put on the stopwatch on your phone."

As soon as we were ready, Asher placed the call.

He gave Simone a small nod the moment the call went through. "Zio, I have to talk fast. We found something. A box." I leaned across the aisle to listen as he described the box and what had happened to us.

"Nothing?" he asked after a moment of listening to his uncle. "What about what the blind woman said about opening it when we can't see? Do you know what that might mean?" Asher listened to his uncle for a few seconds. "Well, I know it's a riddle of some kind." Another beat. "Yes, of course, you need to see the box, but we're not nearby and—"

I could see Asher's entire body tensing up after being interrupted. "Yes, I'm keeping an eye on her, but I don't think she'll go back."

"Fifteen seconds left," I whispered. "Ask him about my father."

Through the phone I could hear Brother Gregorio speaking harshly. It wasn't the attitude he had shown while we were at the monastery.

"Ask about my dad," I insisted.

"Have you heard anything about Cassie's father?" he asked, then shook his head no.

I could hear Brother Gregorio still talking, but Asher now turned his back to me.

Something was going on.

"Time," I whispered as the stopwatch app hit forty-five seconds.

Asher nodded, but kept talking. He had dropped his voice, but I could still pick out a few words here and there. A very defiant "there has to be another way" and "what if I can't?" followed up with a resigned "I understand."

He had to hang up. The call was going on fifty-five seconds and was going to get traced. "Time!" I said again and shook Asher by the shoulder.

"Done," he said, turning off the phone and quickly removing the battery.

"He didn't know anything about the box or my dad, did he?" I asked.

Asher sighed. "No. He'll look through his books, but he's never heard of a box like what Signora Pescatori gave us."

"What if we call someone else? An expert," Simone suggested, not looking up from her phone.

"No one is a bigger expert on the spear than my uncle," Asher said matter-of-factly.

"But what about an expert on boxes?" Simone bit the edge of her fingernail. "I mean, I can't find anything on the Internet, but"—she paused for a moment—"you know, my mom has access to a lot of people. She *could* help."

"Your mom?" Simone was not one to turn to her mother for help . . . on anything. Maybe the half-eared guy had scared her a lot more than she let on.

"Absolutely not!" Asher shook his head. "We don't tell anyone until Zio sees it. Once we get to Orvieto we have to head directly back to the monastery. No other choice."

I stared at the box. The clue was there, waiting for me to find it. "I'm not doing either of those things," I said.

"Then what's the plan?" Simone asked.

"I'm not sure," I admitted. "I just know that we have to try to figure this out ourselves. We have some time before we get to Orvieto, and if we don't know something by then, we can go do research at the town's library."

"All right. But if we don't have any answers by tonight, we go back to the monastery," Asher said.

"Or call my mother," Simone added.

I wasn't going to argue. We would figure this out, because there wasn't any other choice. My dad's safety depended on it.

Maybe that's where I would find a clue. With my dad.

"My dad's notebook!" I panicked, realizing that I'd given it to Asher back in Civita. "Asher, please say you still have it."

"Of course." He pulled it out of his hoodie's pocket and handed it to me.

I let out a long sigh. So far we hadn't found any other clues in the journal, but that didn't mean they weren't there.

"You think he might have written something about the box?" Simone asked.

"I don't know, maybe," I said and flipped open the notebook. There was another side to my father, one that I didn't know. One that kept secrets. I needed to find out more about who he really was. Turning to the very first page, I read his entries again, not for information about the spear or me, but for clues about him.

I was still reading the first few entries when the bus abruptly got dark. We had entered a tunnel, and I could no longer see what I was reading. It would take only a few seconds to exit, but the wait still bothered me. Then, out of the corner of my eye, there was a slight glimmer. I looked down. A faint glow was coming from the top of the box. The gold paint on the pinwheel was radiating, creating a cross from four of the wedges. Inside the right wedge, a string of numbers faintly appeared. It was like looking at the stars, where you could see more by not staring directly at them.

"Simone," I whispered, not taking my eyes off the box. "Simone."

"Give me a sec." She was reading something on her phone. I could make out the number forty-one. "SIMONE!"

"What?" she asked. She looked over just as the bus popped out of the tunnel and back into the sunlight. In the daylight, the box returned to normal.

"The box. It was glowing and there were numbers written over here." I touched the now plain-looking wedge of the pinwheel.

"I saw it, too!" Asher said. "And the gold along these red triangles"—he reached over and traced four of the wedges—"they form the Maltese Cross. I don't know how I didn't notice before."

"The Maltese Cross?" Simone slowly repeated Asher's words.

"Yes! It's the symbol for the Knights of Malta," Asher explained. "That's a really big clue."

Hope and excitement filled my chest. "It's what Signora Pescatori meant by not opening it until we couldn't see. There's stuff written in some type of invisible, glow-in-the-dark paint. I bet there's more inside the box."

"Okay." Simone slowly nodded. "I get it. It has to be dark for the clues to appear."

"Right." I looked around, but there was no place to go inside the bus. "When we get to Orvieto, we need to find someplace dark to look at the box again." I reached over and clutched Simone's hand. "We're going to find this spear and make everything right. I just know it."

Simone gave me a halfhearted smile. She wasn't so convinced.

—NINETEEN—

As soon as the bus stopped, the three of us jumped out of our seats. We had arrived in Orvieto, but I didn't care about the city. From the bus's window I had already spotted a door for a storage closet near the corner of the bus station building.

"Let's go!" I said, pushing aside a few of the passengers.

Once outside, I raced over to the closet and tried opening it, but it was locked.

"Let's look for somewhere inside the station," Asher suggested, the backpack under his arm.

"Don't bother." Simone was a few feet away, holding open a nearby door. "I found a place."

We hurried over, but Asher abruptly stopped. "The women's restroom? Are you serious? You want me to go in there?"

"It's dark and empty." Simone put a hand on her hip. "You have a problem with it?"

Asher paused, then went inside. Simone gave me a mischievous smile.

"You are so bad sometimes," I whispered as I passed Simone.

Simone cocked her head to the side and gave me a wink. "I try to be."

A motion-sensor turned on the overhead light as we entered, but I could see that there were no windows—it would go dark if we stood still.

"Man, this place really smells." Simone pinched her nose.

The smell of old urine was overwhelming. "Even for a bus station, this is pretty bad."

"Figures, since you found it," Asher answered.

"And what is that supposed to mean?" Simone took a step closer to Asher.

Asher threw his hands up in mock surrender. "Ooh, I'm scared."

"Guys!" I shouted. "Please stop moving or the light will never shut off."

For the next couple of minutes none of us spoke or moved. *Click.*

The lights turned off. The room was plunged into complete darkness except for a crack of light that came from underneath the door.

Immediately, the outline of the Maltese Cross glowed on the wooden box, and the numbers appeared much clearer than when we were on the bus.

41.88346, 12.47837

"They could be coordinates," Simone whispered.

I ran my fingers over the numbers. "Write them down."

"I am," Simone answered, entering them into the phone. "Go ahead and open the box."

"Okay, here goes." I held my breath and lifted the lid. Inside, on the bottom of the box, where nothing had appeared in the daylight, was a poem written in elegant and ornate script.

In the garden of my heart
A dagger found its mark

Slicing through the cross's core
Casting me to the dark

There was no doubt in my mind. These words were telling us where the spear was hidden. I flipped the box over and searched for other secret messages, but nothing else was there.

My thoughts wandered to all the medieval art I'd seen with my dad. "The poem might be referring to someone, maybe in a painting or a statue, whose heart is being pierced."

Asher spoke. "Like the pierced hearts of Jesus or Mary that you see in some of the churches."

"The dagger could be the spear. Maybe the spear is hidden wherever this painting or statue is. We just have to locate the right one." I was getting excited at the idea of being so close.

"Only one way of finding out." Simone walked toward the door, and the light clicked back on.

"What are you doing?" I asked. I stuffed the box into the backpack and followed her outside.

"No reason to stay in there any longer than necessary. Plus, look." She showed me her phone. "If the numbers are coordinates, they line up with a place called the Priorato di Malta in Rome."

"Malta . . ." I traced the gold on the lid. "Like the Maltese Cross."

"Oh, no." A look of dread covered Asher's face, when he should have been happy at the discovery.

"What?" I asked.

"It's the Knights of Malta compound," he explained. "Getting in there is . . . *complicated*."

"Why?" Simone asked. "By the looks of it"—she touched the screen, making the image larger—"it's right in the middle of Rome. Even close to a metro station."

"It is, but it's more of a country within a country. The compound is even recognized by the United Nations."

"Like the Vatican?" I asked.

"Not quite, but similar." Asher ran his fingers through his hair. It reminded me of what my father would do. "They have their own coins, passports . . . all the things a sovereign country has."

"So? Are these Knights going to challenge us to a joust or something?" Simone said sarcastically. "What's the big deal? Can't we go visit like average tourists?"

"You don't get it. Most Knights know nothing about the spear and its secrets, but a few that live in the compound do. And they definitely don't like the Hastati."

"Well, that could be good for us, then," Simone stated. "We're not big fans of the Hastati, either."

Asher shook his head. "It's not good if you are Hastati . . ." He lifted his hand, showing off his ring while pointing to my finger. "Or if like Cassie and me, you happen to be wearing a ring they gave you."

—TWENTY—

I didn't care what the Knights thought about the Hastati or about the fact that I wore some ring. The answer, and possibly the spear, was somewhere in that compound, and no one would stop me from going there. The first train back to Rome left at three fifteen, which gave us about twenty minutes to buy our tickets and grab some sandwiches to take with us.

"I'll be right back," Simone announced as we stepped into a small café next to the train station. "I need to visit a cleaner restroom than the one we were in."

I scanned the café to make sure nothing seemed out of place or suspicious. There were a couple of people at a table near the door, and one man, wearing shabby clothes, was slumped over a small round table in the very back. He was either napping or sleeping off a drunken stupor. It looked relatively safe, but, just in case, I wanted to get moving.

"Simone, what do you want?" I called out.

"Anything." She pulled open the door to the ladies' room in the back and disappeared.

The prepared sandwiches were lined up in the refrigerated glass case. Although my stomach grumbled at the sight of the food, I didn't feel like eating anything.

I stole a quick glance at the front door, almost expecting one of our pursuers to show up. We needed to hurry.

Out of the corner of my eye, I caught Asher staring at me. "What?" I asked.

"Nothing. Just thinking about stuff." Asher shoved his hands into the pockets of his hoodie. "Something my uncle said."

"What?"

He looked back at the food. "It's complicated." He pointed to the sandwiches. "Prosciutto okay?"

"Sure." I wanted to know what Brother Gregorio had said, but I needed to play it smart. He wasn't going to just tell me.

I twisted the Hastati ring once, twice, three times around my finger. You would think that if it had slipped over my knuckle when I put it on, it would be able to come off the same way. There was no reason why it should be this stuck.

Asher grabbed my hand. "Do you want to die? Leave it alone."

"Yeah, right, *it's* going to kill me." I picked up the sandwiches. "C'mon, tell the truth. Why does Brother Gregorio want the two of us wearing them? Are they tracking devices? Is that why he wanted to get one for Simone, too?"

"No." He stared at his own ring before taking out his wallet.

"But they both do the same thing?" It felt like I was pulling teeth in order to get any answers.

"Yeah."

There was a heaviness in his one-word answers. I'd thought he was exaggerating when he said the ring could kill me, but now I wasn't so sure. I leaned in closer. "Don't make me ask a thousand questions, Asher. Just tell me why we can't take them off."

"Because." He looked away. "It's complicated."

"Again with the complicated! I'm really starting to hate that word." This whole conversation was getting me angry. "Nothing is complicated if you explain it."

"Cassie, there are some things that are best unknown."

"I trusted you with my dad's journal; you need to trust me with whatever you know. I promise I won't tell anyone."

Asher stared at me, then rubbed the back of his neck. I could see he was having an internal debate about something. He took three sodas from the counter, paid, and motioned for me to follow him over to a far corner. "I pretty much already told you," he said in a low voice, though there was no one around to hear us.

"No, all you said was that if I took off the ring I'd die."

"Yeah, because that's what the rings are for."

"Huh?" I was confused. "You want me to believe that your uncle gave us these rings so he could kill us?"

Asher sighed. "He doesn't want to, but he'll do it if he has to."

My face must have said it all, because I couldn't speak.

"Don't look at me like that. He isn't a bad guy."

"Oh, really? Asher, you just said that the person my dad and I were trusting . . . the person who's supposed to keep me *safe* from Hastati assassins . . . is willing to kill me. And willing to kill you, his own nephew. What kind of face am I supposed to have?"

He shook his head. "This is why it's complicated. He would only do it in a worst-case situation. If we had the spear and got caught or something, so that we wouldn't be forced to use it to choose the wrong destiny. To prevent us from being turned into weapons."

"Fine. Even if he'd do this to me . . ." I paused. "Why you? You're family. There's no reason to get you involved in all of this."

"That's what you don't get. I have no choice. My uncle has no choice. It's our duty. Our heritage. It's why he's had me training ever since I moved to Rome. When he told me about the spear and the Hastati, he had to make sure I wouldn't tell anyone. That's when—"

"When you got the ring." I finished his sentence.

He bit his lip and nodded.

I inched closer to him, still keeping an eye out for anyone who might come into the café. "But can't we just cut it off?"

"It has a poison inside. If you cut the ring or take it off in the wrong way, a tiny needle pricks you. You'll be dead, or in a coma, within seconds. I don't know all the details because I'm still a novice. I'm supposed to find out everything by the time I'm eighteen, but you came along a little earlier." He took a deep breath. "I probably shouldn't even be telling you all this."

"So how—"

Asher shook his head, and I noticed his attention was on something behind me. I turned to see Simone walking over.

She had a strange look on her face. "What are you two talking about?" She took one of the sodas from Asher's hands.

"Um, nothing really," I said. "We were just going over the stuff we already know." I hated lying to her, but it felt important that Asher trust me.

"Hm, from over there it seemed like it was a little more intense than that, but whatever." She looked down at the can and made a face. "They didn't have anything diet?"

"You didn't ask for that," Asher said.

"Cassie knows I only drink diet." She turned to me. "Did you forget?"

"I didn't order." There were bigger things to worry about than drinking a few extra calories. "We should get going. The train will be here soon."

"Uh-huh. So, these Knights of Malta . . . are they real knights?" Simone asked as we headed out.

"What do you mean?" Asher held the door open for us. "Are you asking whether they wear chain-mail armor and cover their heads with a big metal helmet?" He paused. "The answer to that would be no."

"Ha-ha. Very funny." Simone walked out. "I mean I've heard of the Knights Templar, but never the Knights of Malta."

"Yeah, movies like to focus a lot on the Templars," Asher said. "The Knights of Malta fought battles at one time, too, but now they pretty much run hospitals and clinics. Do charity work."

"So why do they hate the Hastati?" I asked.

"It's a long story."

"We have a few minutes before the train gets here," Simone said. "Tell us."

"It goes back a long time. The Knights and Hastati never got along. They each thought it was their responsibility to guard the spear. Neither trusted the other, so the spear kept being traded between the two groups. Eventually, it was agreed that the Hastati would keep the spear, but the Knights would decide who could use it. Then, about twelve years ago, after the spear went missing and the Hastati decided to eliminate anyone with the birthmark—"

"You mean *kill* anyone with a birthmark," Simone said. "Don't sugarcoat it, Asher. Don't pretend that the Hastati aren't ruthless killers."

"Yeah, well, one of the marked descendants the Hastati ended up killing was a high-ranking Knight. The Knights were already opposed to what the Hastati were doing, but that really got them angry. Now the two groups won't even speak to each other anymore."

"So if the Knights don't like the Hastati, maybe we can convince them to help us," I said.

"What if they're the ones who stole the spear in the first place?" Simone pointed out. "Then they wouldn't want us to find it."

Asher shot down Simone's theory. "I don't think they have it—why would they have let one of their own be killed if they already had the spear?"

"People have done stranger things," Simone mused.

"Well, we'll find out soon enough." I pointed to a train approaching the station. "Let's go pay them a visit."

*   *   *

The train rumbled as it passed through the Italian landscape on its way to Rome. Simone had given me the throwaway phone to look up as much information as I could on the Knights and the clues we'd found. As I read about the history of the Knights, Simone simply stared out the window.

"Hey, you okay?" I tapped her on the shoulder. "You've been acting weird since lunch."

"I'm fine." She took a deep breath, but didn't look at me. "My stomach is acting up, that's all."

"Want me to get you something? I can see if there's dining service in one of the other train cars."

"No, I can take care of myself." She said this with a sharpness that she usually reserved for others. A second later she turned to look at me. "Sorry. I don't make a very good sick person. Why don't you tell me what you found? It'll get my mind off my stomach."

"Nothing about getting into the compound. Seems like they only allow visitors in by advance request, although tourists line up to visit the outside and look through a keyhole in the gate. Supposedly, the dome of the Vatican lines up perfectly through the keyhole. It's considered one of Rome's 'secrets,' though I can't imagine it being cool enough to make it into most tour books."

"Well, I'd never heard of it, and I've been living in Rome for a few years now."

I was starting to come up with an idea. "Maybe if we pretend to be tourists or students doing a project we can get inside the compound. Look around and find another clue."

"Maybe," Simone repeated, turning to look out the window again.

Asher popped his head over the seat in front of us. "We'll be in Rome in a few minutes. It might be best to go to the Knights' compound without telling my uncle anything about it. He may say we can't go."

"It's better that way." I twisted the ring around my finger before remembering that there was poison inside. I had to stop touching it. "The less other people know what we're doing, the safer we are. We just need to make sure that whatever we find out stays between the three of us."

"Agreed," Asher said.

Simone said nothing, continuing to stare out the window.

"Something wrong, Simone?" Asher asked.

"Huh? Oh, no, nothing's wrong." She pointed up ahead to the warehouses riddled with graffiti that bordered the four or five different train tracks. "I was just noticing that we're almost there."

"Yeah, I kinda said that ten seconds ago."

Simone glared at him. "Well, excuse me if I don't hang on your every word. Didn't realize I had to pay such close attention to you." She shifted her body so that half her back was to Asher and she could keep looking out the window.

"Her stomach is messed up," I explained, watching Asher's startled expression.

He shook his head and muttered, "That's not all that's messed up."

—TWENTY-ONE—

Once in Rome, it was only a short ride on the metro to the Circo Massimo stop. As we came out of the underground station, I noticed how the day had taken on a golden haze. There wasn't much time before nightfall, and my plan of sneaking in with a group of tourists might hit a snag if it was too late in the day and the compound was closed. We walked quickly along the tree-lined gravel footpath that separated us from the speeding cars on the left and the ancient ruins of the Roman racetrack on the right. My heart fluttered every time a motorcyclist zoomed past us, but for the time being it appeared that we had managed to throw our two assassins off our scent.

"Go through there. It's a shortcut." Asher pointed to a bike path that went through the middle of the park on the opposite side of the street. "Plus, we won't be so visible."

Darting between cars, we crossed and made our way through the park onto Via di Santa Sabina. The quiet street was flanked on the right side by a large brick wall and the left alternated between parking lots, narrow side streets, or the back side of buildings. I had read that the compound was at the very top of Aventine Hill, one of Rome's seven hills, and I could feel the slope of the street getting stronger.

"Is that it?" Simone was looking through a wrought-iron fence that closed off a small park and church. About a

162

hundred yards away, past a few benches and a scattering of trees, I could see Rome's skyline. Red clay rooftops and different hues of peach-colored buildings stood out against the cloudy sky.

"No. The compound is farther down . . . at the very end of the street." Asher adjusted the backpack's strap on his shoulder. "Over there." He pointed to where the street dead-ended at a small courtyard. People were lined up in front of a pair of massive doors: the entrance to the Priorato di Malta.

I let out a huge sigh of relief. We'd made it in time. Now we needed to blend in with the other tourists.

I quietly walked around the courtyard, watching each person take their turn looking through the "secret" keyhole. I'd hoped to find a group with reservations to see the inside of the compound and sneak in with them, but it didn't seem like any of these people were going inside. I tilted my head up to look at the huge perimeter wall, which made the compound more of a fortress. My backup plan had been to climb over the wall, but it was at least twenty feet tall.

As the last of the tourists left the area and headed back down the street, the three of us immediately went over to the door. On the upper corner of the gate, I spotted a small security camera. Someone was watching us.

"So what now?" Asher asked, bending down to put his eye against the keyhole.

I stayed silent for a couple of moments. Both of my plans had fallen apart.

Asher straightened up and took a step away from the door. "I don't see anyone in there. Either of you have any ideas?"

"Let me look." Simone peered through the keyhole.

"We could knock," I suggested.

"Knock?" Simone turned her head to look at me. "Just knock?"

"Yeah." I was forming a new plan. "We knock to get their attention, then show them the box through the camera. It's our bait. They'll either think it's a delivery or they'll know exactly what the box is. Either way, someone will come to the door and when they do then—"

"Then Asher can rush them!" Simone stood up with a twinkle in her eye.

"I'm not an attack dog that you sic on people." Asher leaned against the door. "But it could work. Although I suggest we give them a chance to let us in before forcing ourselves inside." He pulled the box from his backpack, keeping his left hand in his pocket. "Make sure you don't let them see your ring, Cassie."

I had already carefully twisted the ring around so all that could be seen was the plain silver band. With my right hand I slammed the metal door knocker several times, creating loud echoing bangs in the stillness of the courtyard. The three of us waited. Asher lifted the box toward the camera in case anyone was zooming in on us.

Nothing happened.

The door remained closed, and we were still no closer to getting inside.

Simone looked through the keyhole again, then tried to fit her pinkie into the opening. "If only we had something that could pick this lock."

"A key," I muttered. Signora Pescatori had told us about a key. What had she said? I tried to think of the exact words.

The key is in the eye of the beholder.

Maybe it had something to do with my eye. The way I saw things.

"Scoot over," I told Simone. "Let me look through it."

The keyhole was deep, not allowing me to see much except for what was directly ahead, but what I could see was exactly as described in the guidebooks. A line of cypress trees inside the compound formed a tunnel to the edge of the hill, and at the other end, in the distance, was the Vatican dome. It did create a very pretty picture.

A burst of light flashed in my eye, and I jumped back.

"What is it?" Asher asked.

I blinked, still seeing the blue-white line. "A light. Like someone taking a picture."

Simone checked the keyhole again. "Nothing happens when I look through it."

I nodded. "I thought I might see something different because I'm the one with the birthmark. Signora Pescatori said the key was in the eye of the beholder." I glanced up at the camera again. "I didn't think it would try to blind me."

"Curiouser and curiouser," Simone mumbled.

"What?" Asher asked.

"Just a line from a book," Simone said. "It feels like we're falling through a rabbit hole."

"I have no idea what you're talking about, but if—"

Asher shut up as the door creaked open. A large man wearing a dark suit, white shirt, and skinny black tie stood there looking at the three of us. He was bigger than a body-builder and had less of a neck. *"Tu."* He pointed to me. *"Seguimi. Gli altri aspettano qui."*

He wanted me to follow him inside. "And my friends?" I asked.

His cold stare sent a shiver up my spine. "In English, then," he said with a very thick accent. "Only you. The grand con-sigliere wishes to see you. The others wait here."

"No." Asher stepped in front of me. "She doesn't go in alone." It didn't seem to matter to Asher that this man dwarfed him in height and width.

The man cracked his knuckles. He may have been wear-ing a suit, but his business was not sitting behind a desk. He was some type of guard. To stress this fact, he slowly pulled his jacket to the side, revealing a gun holster.

"Then she can stay out here with you," he answered, plac-ing a hand on the door as if to close it.

"Wait." Simone eased Asher back and spoke directly to the guard. "I know your boss doesn't want Cassie to go away," she said with a certain authority in her voice. "If she leaves, it'll be your responsibility, and that may get you into some serious trouble." She paused for emphasis. "And no one wants any trouble, right?" Simone had his attention. She was good at this type of thing. "So why don't you go inside and explain that we are a package deal. We all come in, or we all go home. We'll give you a few minutes to get us an answer."

The guard's jaw tensed up, and his eyes narrowed. "Fine. Stay here."

He closed the door with a large thud.

"That was awesome," I whispered to Simone, giving her a little nudge. "You totally got him to back down."

Simone smiled. I could see she was proud of herself.

"Have to admit," Asher said reluctantly, "you did sound pretty convincing. Guess you've picked up a few things from your mother."

"That was all me . . . not my mother," she clarified. "I wasn't pretending to be her."

Asher shrugged. "Sure, whatever."

"Doesn't matter," I said, not wanting to get distracted by their bickering. "You called his bluff. You did great." I peered through the keyhole again to see if I could see the guard and was quickly blinded once again by the flash. "Ugh." I rubbed my eye. "Stupid light."

"Again?" Simone shook her head and looked through it herself. "I see him. He's walking back."

I felt a twinge of excitement in my chest. This was it. "Okay, if they let us in we have to remember to act like dumb kids on a class assignment so we can check out the place."

"I don't think that idea is going to work anymore, Cassie." Asher returned the box to his backpack and slung the bag over his shoulder. "Based on what just happened, they know that we're not ordinary kids." He tightened his grip on the bag's strap. "We just have to keep our eyes open and not say much. See what they know."

"No." Simone shook her head. "What we need to do is find the spear and get out of here. Cassie isn't safe until we have it."

"Well, yeah." Asher rolled his eyes. "That's what I meant."

"Guys!" I motioned toward the door . . . it was being opened.

"You may all come in," the guard stated. "Follow me." He held the door as we stepped into the compound.

Inside, the area was lush with trees and plants. There were perfectly clipped bushes, rose gardens, and tall cypress trees forming canopied trails in different directions. But there were no paintings or statues with spears or daggers through the heart like the box's poem mentioned. At least none that I could see.

Simone leaned toward me. "Where are we going?" she whispered.

"The consigliere's office," the guard announced, clearly having overheard Simone's question. "She requested to speak with you directly."

"What is a consigliere?" I asked.

"She is an advisor." The guard sounded like he was annoyed with us. "A director of sorts."

We entered a small two-story building. The stone floor of the foyer was inlaid with red marble in the shape of a large Maltese Cross. The guard walked around the design, careful not to step on it, and the three of us followed suit. He stopped in front of a wooden door with a frosted-glass window and knocked.

"Bring them in, Massimo," a woman's voice called out.

The guard opened the door, and we walked in. "The grand consigliere," he said, motioning with his hand to a woman sitting behind an antique wooden desk. "Dame Elisabeth."

She was an older woman with silver hair pulled back in a twist, wearing a dark-blue dress and a pink scarf around her neck. She was attractive, but there was a no-nonsense look to her. There was also something vaguely familiar.

"Welcome," she said, standing up to greet us. "Please have a seat. We have some things to discuss." She turned her attention to the guard. "That will be all, Massimo. Thank you."

Massimo did a curt little bow and backed out of the room, closing the door behind him.

The three of us stood by the door, unsure what to do next. We needed to explore the area, and an administrator's office was not where we needed to start the search.

"Let's begin with your names," Dame Elisabeth said, "and what brings you here."

Simone stepped forward and extended her right hand. "I'm Simone Bimington, and this is Cassie and Asher."

Both Asher and I gave a slight nod.

"Pleasure to meet all of you." Dame Elisabeth shook Simone's hand, but she didn't take her eyes off me. "Cassie, you said?"

"Yes," I answered. "Well, actually it's Cassandra, but everyone calls me Cassie."

"Hmm, Cassandra." She let my name roll off her tongue. It felt as if she were weighing the word, determining its worth. "A good, strong name," she said, still staring at me with a gaze so intense that it felt like she was memorizing my face.

"Um, excuse me, but do you think we might be able to get a tour of the grounds?" Asher asked.

Dame Elisabeth peeled her eyes away from me. "Yes, of course." She arched a single eyebrow and smiled. "Although I believe you are here for more than just a tour."

None of us said anything. We all maintained blank expressions as if we didn't know what she meant.

"My dears, the keyhole confirmed it. We already know Cassandra passed the test."

"Test?" I thought about the flash of light I'd seen while looking through the keyhole.

"Yes, a retinal scanner is hidden in the door. People look through there thinking they are only seeing a pretty picture . . . never realizing that we are looking at them, too." She was staring at me intently again, like I was a bug under a microscope. "Your eye pattern, it's like your birthmark, it identifies you. It tells us you are one of the marked ones. The Knights will now protect you and make sure that the Hastati don't make you a target."

I bristled at the mention of the Hastati. It was enough for Dame Elisabeth to suspect something was wrong.

"Oh," she said. "Have they already targeted you? Do they know of you?"

Simone shook her head. "I think you might have us confused with someone else because—"

Dame Elisabeth raised her hand and cut Simone off. "You've learned not to speak of this nor trust others with the information . . . that's good." She stood up. "But you're not here by coincidence. I've been hoping that one day Cassandra would show up and that I'd be able to give her refuge." She studied our reactions. "That *is* why you're here, correct? Seeking refuge?"

Asher, Simone, and I exchanged a quick glance.

"Yes," we all said in unison.

"Then that is what I will offer you. A safe haven until we can find something more permanent." She walked around the desk and approached Asher. "May I see what you were holding outside?"

Asher took off his backpack, pulled out the box, and handed it to her.

She gazed at it, flipped it over, and ran her fingers along the leaf carvings. "After all these years," Dame Elisabeth muttered. "Where did you find it?" she asked.

"It was given to us," I said. "By a friend."

"I see." Dame Elisabeth clutched the box to her chest, closed her eyes for a moment, and smiled. "This brings back some very special memories."

"Is it yours?" Asher asked.

"No, it was my daughter's." She sighed, and then looked at me. "I'm sorry to keep staring at you, Cassandra," Dame Elisabeth said, her eyes now gentle and soft. "You just look so much like her."

I gave her a slight smile, but all I was thinking was that if the box was her daughter's, then maybe her daughter was the one who hid the spear. We were getting closer to finding it.

"Are you sure the box was hers?" Simone questioned. "It could just be similar."

"Oh, I'm sure," she said, leaning against the desk and setting the box down. "She spent an entire summer here making it herself. I can still see her now, sitting right there working on it." She pointed out the window to a small, perfectly manicured garden with a bench that overlooked the city. In the last few minutes it had grown dark, but a few lampposts lit the area. "She'd be there for hours; it was her favorite spot."

"Is your daughter still here?" Simone asked.

"No." Dame Elisabeth had a pained expression on her face. "She passed away almost thirteen years ago."

"I'm sorry to hear that," I said, disappointed that another link to the spear had disappeared.

Dame Elisabeth scrunched her eyebrows together and gave me a strange look. "I don't understand. Didn't you know? Certainly you knew."

Now it was my turn to be confused.

"Um, no." I shook my head. "How would I know about your daughter?"

"Oh, my." Dame Elisabeth straightened up, cocked her head to the side, and stared at me. "You don't know," she said softly. "I thought that was why you'd come. Because you already knew."

"Knew what?" I asked.

Dame Elisabeth took a few steps and reached for my hand, holding it between both of hers. "Cassandra, my daughter was . . ." She paused for a moment, trying to come up with the right words. "My daughter was your mother. I'm your grandmother."

—TWENTY-TWO—

I pulled my hand away and took a few steps back. It felt like I'd been punched squarely in the gut. *She was my grandmother?* No. That was too crazy to be true. This was a setup. Some type of mind game. This woman wasn't my grandmother. My mother was an orphan. She grew up in foster homes in Cleveland. I didn't have any family except Dad and whoever he had left back in Cuba.

I felt dizzy.

Dame Elisabeth guided me to a chair, her face full of concern. "Are you all right? I didn't mean to shock you."

"Well, what did you expect?" Simone exclaimed, crouching down in front of me. "You can't just announce to someone that you're their grandmother and think they aren't going to be shocked." She waved her hand in front of my face. "Cassie, you okay?"

I nodded, but my head was reeling. This was not the kind of information I thought I'd find in the compound. Growing up, my only link to my mother, besides my father, had been through pictures, and most of those had been lost in one of our many moves. Yet, I still remembered some of my favorites. A close-up of my father and her on their wedding day; a picture of her being very pregnant, eating some ice cream; and, my very favorite, the one where she was smiling, holding me as a newborn, and Papi had his arm around both of us.

"How about some water?" Simone asked.

"Yes, yes. That's a good idea." Dame Elisabeth went around her desk and picked up the phone. "Massimo, bring some water to my office. Quickly."

"No offense," Asher said, standing behind me, "but how do you know Cassie is actually your granddaughter? Just because she reminds you of your daughter, and she has the box, that isn't really proof."

"No, of course that wouldn't be sufficient," she said.

A knock on the door stopped any further discussion. Massimo entered the room holding a silver tray with a pitcher of water and a few glasses.

"Thank you, Massimo," Dame Elisabeth said, serving me a glass. "That'll be all."

"As you wish," he said, eyeing me curiously before leaving the room and closing the door again.

I took a sip of the water and calmed myself down. *Asher was right. This was probably wishful thinking on Dame Elisabeth's part. I couldn't be her granddaughter . . . could I?*

"Feeling better?" Dame Elisabeth asked.

"Yes." I nodded. "But why are you so sure you're my grandmother?"

"Besides the fact that you have the mark, you're the right age, and the uncanny resemblance to your mother . . . I have this." She reached behind her neck, unfastened the gold necklace she was wearing, and opened the locket that hung from the chain.

"Does she look familiar?" she asked, handing it to me.

I looked down at the two photos. The one on the left was the same shot of my mother holding me as a baby that I remembered seeing when I was younger, and the picture on the right was of a much younger Dame Elisabeth with a girl who did bear a striking resemblance to me.

"Your mother sent it to me right after you were born," Dame Elisabeth said. "No return address, just the locket and a note saying you had the mark. It was the last thing she sent me before she passed away."

Could it be true? Was she really my grandmother?

"But you never tried to find me," I said, "or contact me . . . ?"

"It was the only way to protect you. It was why your mother left. To make sure no one came looking for you. I couldn't risk destroying everything she'd sacrificed just to see you." Dame Elisabeth stared out into the night. "I'd warned her about becoming involved with the Hastati, but she wouldn't listen. The night she showed up here and told me she was pregnant . . . we both knew that having her disappear would be the only way to protect you."

"How was she involved with them?" Asher asked.

Dame Elisabeth faced us again. "Perhaps that's a conversation Cassandra and I should have later . . . in private."

The cell phone on her desk rang.

"My friends can hear anything you have to tell me," I said, glancing at both Simone and Asher. "They can be trusted."

"I'm sure, but these are personal matters for me as well." She looked over to see who was calling and grimaced. "I'm sorry. I have to take this call." She picked up the phone and stepped out of the room for privacy.

"What do you think?" Simone whispered to me. "You believe her?"

"I don't know," I said. "It's not the craziest thing I've heard this week. And the photos in the locket are my mother."

"Still, we have to be careful." Asher was riffling through some papers on the desk. "Remember that we're here to find the spear and get it back to my uncle."

Simone had her ear pressed against the door. "She's coming back!" she said in a low voice and darted away as Asher came over to where I was sitting.

When Dame Elisabeth entered the room, we were all in the same places where she'd left us. "I apologize for that interruption, but it seems I have no choice but to leave for a little bit." She seemed a bit more frazzled than when she'd left. "In the meantime, you can stay here, and I'll have Massimo bring you some dinner." She pulled out a small key from her pocket and opened a locked drawer in her desk.

This was good news. We were going to be left alone, which meant we'd have a chance to search for the spear. I didn't want to even look at Simone or Asher to see if they were thinking the same thing I was. "That's fine," I said. "But is there a restroom we could use?"

"Oh, of course." She pulled out a file and closed the drawer again while her cell phone buzzed. She checked it and scowled. "I'll have Massimo show you." She opened the door of her office. "Massimo!" Dame Elisabeth called out. "Massimo!"

Her cell phone was buzzing again.

"I don't know where he is right now," she said, speaking very quickly. "But here, I'll just tell you where to go. Come."

We followed her out into the hallway.

"See those stairs?" she said, pointing to a marble staircase. "Go up to the second floor and make a left. The restrooms are on the right-hand side of the hallway. Afterward, just return to my office. I shouldn't be too long." She turned on her heel to leave, then swiveled around to face me, putting her hands on my shoulders. "I really am very glad to finally meet you, Cassandra. We'll fill each other in as soon as I get back, okay?"

"Sure, no problem," I said, anxious to start searching the compound for the spear. This may have been my grandmother, but I was here to save my dad.

Dame Elisabeth smiled and tucked a lock of hair behind my ear. "So much like your mother," she muttered.

"Cassie, are you coming?" Simone asked. I looked to see Simone waiting for me by the stairs and Asher heading up.

"Yeah." I turned to catch up with them.

"Don't leave the Priorato, Cassandra," Dame Elisabeth shouted. "It's not safe out there for you."

"You have no idea," I said under my breath.

But, no matter the danger, I knew I'd leave the moment I found that spear.

—TWENTY-THREE—

"Never trust the Knights," Asher said once we regrouped at the top of the stairs. "My uncle always told me this and he was right. We have to stick together."

"I agree." Simone nodded emphatically. "Plus, what do we really know about this Dame Elisabeth?"

We didn't have time to discuss this. "We'll never be able to cover the whole compound if we don't split up," I argued.

"It's not safe," Asher insisted. "Someone could still attack you here."

Simone bit her nail. "What if Cassie and I stay inside the building while you go out? That way we aren't completely exposed."

It was a good compromise. "C'mon, Asher," I said. "We're already wasting time."

Asher hesitated, but then relented. "Fine."

"Plus"—Simone smiled—"if someone gets caught it'll only be you."

Asher glared at her. "I won't get caught." He grabbed the banister and pointed at me. "Twenty minutes," he said, and then leapt down to the next landing before disappearing around the corner.

"Simone, do you want to check this floor while I go downstairs and look around?"

"Works for me. If your grandmother comes back, just say I'm in the bathroom."

I nodded and headed down the stairs.

If everything Dame Elisabeth said was true, my mother used to roam these halls . . . and she made the box with the riddle. It seemed like she was even the one who hid the spear . . . but where?

Every room downstairs seemed to be an office, and none had statues or spears. I walked back into Dame Elisabeth's office and looked out the window. Asher was out there somewhere, but all I could see was the entrance to what had been my mom's favorite garden.

Garden. The first line of the poem talked about the garden of her heart.

My mother was talking about her favorite garden.

That must be where she hid the spear!

I had to get Simone and go search outside. Racing out of the room, I overheard some voices arguing from down the hall. One of them was Dame Elisabeth, and she sounded upset.

I tiptoed over to the closed door.

"I should've been informed earlier." Dame Elisabeth's tone had a hard edge to it. "The moment he took a turn for the worse."

"It was unconfirmed rumors," an unfamiliar, gruff voice responded. "But now the girl is in more danger. Do you want to tell her about her father's condition?" he asked.

My ears perked up and my heart started beating harder. It

took extra effort just to hear them over the pounding in my chest.

"Eventually," Dame Elisabeth answered. "Right now, she seems a bit overwhelmed."

"He may have less than an hour." The man's voice was very matter-of-fact. "We need to start preparing."

My knees buckled, but I braced myself against the wall. *No, no, NO!* My father couldn't die. This couldn't be happening. There had to be a way to save him. I had to do something.

"Maybe," I muttered to myself. "Maybe I can save him."

An idea took root. *The spear. If I had it . . . if I could somehow activate it . . . I could use it to change destiny. To change my father's fate. I just needed to find it—fast.*

I charged toward the front door, pulled it open, and ran outside.

The path to the garden was lit by small lamps, but otherwise the area was shrouded in darkness, with tall cypress trees providing cover from any prying eyes. The area had neatly trimmed hedges and a concrete bench at the far end that overlooked the city of Rome down below. I thought about the poem.

> *In the garden of my heart*
> *A dagger found its mark*
> *Slicing through the cross's core*
> *Casting me to the dark*

The dagger in the second line of the poem was probably code for the spear, but what did it mean to be slicing the cross's core?

"What cross?" I whispered, spinning around and not seeing any crosses in the garden. I gazed out past the rooftops of Rome. Even at night, the city lights showed several churches that had domes or bell towers with crosses perched on top. Could the poem be sending me to one of them?

My heart fell. There was no way I'd find the spear in time to change my father's fate if I had to go to all those churches.

No. There *had* to be another answer.

I stood on top of the bench to see farther out. I had to find another clue. A sign pointing me in the right direction.

But there was nothing.

Maybe if Asher and Simone helped. As I was about to jump off the bench, I noticed the pattern of the hedges in the garden. When looking at it from above, the shrubs formed a perfect Maltese Cross, and in the center, where the four wedges met, was a stepping-stone much darker than all the others.

The cross's core cast in the dark. That was it. The spear had to be buried there!

I jumped off the bench and cut through the hedge to get to the center. Dropping to the ground, I grasped the edges of the flat stone and pushed it to the side.

I dug down into the moist soil. About four inches down, a piece of blue velvet poked out from the ground.

It was here! I'd really found it!

Clawing at the ground faster, I uncovered a small bundle of velvet that had been lying only inches beneath where people walked every day. Lifting it out of the ground, I unwrapped the cloth to reveal a somewhat tarnished, ordinary-looking spearhead.

I remembered Asher's warning about touching the spear. I'd promised not to do it, but this was an emergency. The last thing I wanted to do was become bound to it for life, but if this was the only way to save my dad, I'd do it.

My hands trembled.

No one had to know that I'd used the spear. If it worked, I promised myself, I'd never use it again.

"Get it together, Cassie," I whispered. "You were born to do this."

There were no instructions on how to make it work or how to choose a different destiny; I just had to go with my gut and hope for the best.

I took a deep breath and wrapped my dirty fingers tightly around the spear. Its metal was cool to the touch. *Please*, I prayed, *let this work*.

I waited, but nothing happened. Maybe there was too much dirt for it to work. I ran to a nearby fountain and rinsed my hands and the spear, then wiped it dry with my shirt.

I tried again, rubbing it as if it were Aladdin's lamp, wishing for my dad to be healthy.

Still, nothing happened.

A sinking feeling formed in the middle of my chest. Brother Gregorio had said that only one person could be bound at any given time—and they'd been using Tobias to trap the power. Maybe he still had it. Or maybe I wasn't who everyone thought I was. Either way, it meant that I wasn't going to save my dad.

It was over. I had failed.

I slumped to the ground . . . defeated. I'd tried so hard to be brave, but now I could feel tears starting to run down my face.

Opening my messenger bag, I shoved the spear inside. Just as I was about to drop it in, I felt a slight tingle, like a small current, hit my fingertips. At first I thought it was my cell phone, but I didn't have one with me. My heart raced. I clasped the spear harder, afraid to let go.

There was a blinding light, like if I had stared into the sun. I wanted to cover my eyes, but I couldn't move. It was as if I had been removed from my body, so I was no longer sitting next to the fountain or in the compound or anywhere in Rome. I was somewhere else, in neither darkness nor light, but surrounding me there was a vast stretch of nothingness. It was the strangest sensation. It felt like there were limitless possibilities, only I couldn't see any of them.

Then, like a vacuum sucking me down into existence, I was back inside my body. My eyes were closed, and my breathing had slowed down. The blood coursing through my veins made an incredibly loud whooshing noise in my ears.

Faces and images flew all around me.

Focus, I told myself. *You need to find your father.*

Suddenly, it all stopped. A group of doctors and nurses surrounding a hospital bed were frantically working on a patient. I wasn't sure how I knew it was my father, but I could feel our connection, the fact that his blood flowed through my veins.

And there was a sound. A long monotone beep.

One of the doctors stepped back, shook his head, and whipped off his medical gloves. I was too late.

My father was dead.

—TWENTY-FOUR—

"NO!" I yelled, opening my eyes and looking at the spear still in my grasp. There had to be another choice. What good was the power to change destiny if I couldn't change my father's fate?

There was no way I was going to give up. I closed my eyes and concentrated harder. I fell back into the void, but this time I sensed that I was drifting forward, almost like a surfer on a gentle wave. On the horizon, I could see what looked to be a cemetery. If I did nothing, I'd continue travelling with the current toward the tombstone, but that wasn't where I wanted to go. There had to be another choice. I calmed my breathing. I was clueless on how to change what I'd seen, but I wasn't going to stop trying.

"He can't die. He has to wake up and be fine," I whispered to myself and to whatever power I was accessing. "Make it happen."

A narrow channel unfolded in my mind's eye. It was like an undercurrent, going in a different direction than the wave I was surfing. I focused on that undercurrent, trying to follow the connection with my father. I wanted to see where this path would take me. A scene appeared in the distance, like looking at one of those old flickering movies. A doctor was yelling at the nurses to stand back. I willed myself forward, gliding toward that image. The long monotone beep I'd heard earlier suddenly started to beep in a rhythm. My father's heart was pumping again.

I'd done it. I'd saved him!

But I didn't know where he was.

"I need to know where he is," I muttered, figuring that the last time I said something the spear helped me save my dad. "Show me when I'll be with him."

Images spun again like a fast-moving merry-go-round and finally settled on an unfamiliar man looking out toward a brilliant blue sea.

This was not what I wanted. Maybe I hadn't been clear on who I wanted to be with. "No, no, my father, Felipe Arroyo. I need to be with him. Show me when that will happen."

I felt myself being pulled at blinding speed somewhere else. Then I stopped, and there was an image of my father in a hospital room. Outside, there was a flash of lightning and the sound of thunder. Through a blurry window I could see a white car driving away. I tried to get a clue of where we were, but the image was fading. I heard my father say "*m'ija*," and I noticed a digital clock on the wall that showed the date and time. It was tomorrow morning at 11:58.

Suddenly, I was being hurtled through space again. Now the images were coming at me faster. All I could see was a hand holding a gun, and I heard muffled voices arguing until a shot was fired. That vision was quickly replaced with one of several people in hazmat suits walking down a city street, which instantly blended into bodies . . . dead, rotting bodies, scattered along the same street, with a fire burning in a nearby park. The images kept picking up speed. Thousands of them seemed to be flying by me so fast that I couldn't make sense of any of them. I felt myself propelled forward . . . faster and faster. Everything around me was turning into a blur. I was out of control. I needed to get to the present, but I didn't know how. In this place I had no voice, no body, but I could feel my heart speeding up. I couldn't breathe. I was gasping for air.

It felt like I was going to die.

"Cassie?" I could hear Asher, but he sounded far away. "Cassie!"

There was a touch on my shoulder. It felt like an electric current shocking me back into reality. My eyes popped open in time to see Asher stumble.

"What was that?" he asked. He was flicking his hand wildly.

"I don't know," I said, dropping the spear into my bag. I couldn't tell him about what I'd just done.

"You okay?" He crouched down next to me.

I nodded and pushed the hair away from my face.

He reached over, his fingertips lightly touching my cheek. "Were you crying?"

I felt the tracks left behind by my tears.

"What happened?" he asked. "Why did you come outside?"

"I . . . I was looking for you," I said, trying to quickly come up with a story to explain how I'd gotten the spear.

"But you were just sitting here."

"Yeah. I thought I heard Massimo . . . I didn't want him to spot me."

Even in the darkness, I could tell that Asher didn't believe me. "Then how did you expect me to find you?"

"Doesn't matter, you found me, right?" I needed to change the subject. "We need to grab Simone and get out of here." I tapped my messenger bag. "I got the spear. My grandmother gave it to me, but we have to leave before anyone finds out."

Asher froze. Instead of smiling, his face contorted and I could see the rage building in his eyes. "You didn't. Ugh!" He grabbed the top of his hair and pulled on it. "You promised you wouldn't touch it. Now . . . now everything is messed up!"

"No, Dame Elisabeth knew I couldn't touch it." I was talking as fast I was thinking. "She slipped it into the bag. I haven't done anything."

"Give me the bag," he demanded. "You shouldn't even be close to it." He paused while I slipped off the strap and handed it to him. His eyes narrowed. "I know you're lying."

"I'm not," I said, but he wasn't listening.

He stared at his own hands. "And now you've dragged me down with you," he muttered. "Not that I could've done it anyway."

"Done what?"

"My duty, Cassie!" he said through clenched teeth. "The one thing I was supposed to do and . . ." He shoved his hands into his pockets. "I failed. I can't do it!"

"Asher, I don't know what you're talking about, but if it has to do with the spear"—I crossed my fingers—"I promise I didn't touch it."

He turned his back on me and took a couple of steps.

I knew it was stupid to cross my fingers, like a little kid, but it somehow made me feel better. This was a necessary lie.

"I want to believe you. I really do," he said without turning around. "It would make everything so much easier."

"Then believe me."

"What you don't understand is that—"

"Cassie!" Simone was running at full speed over to us. "I was so worried when I couldn't find you inside." She threw her arms around my neck and hugged me. "What are you two doing out here? Why didn't you come get me?"

"I have the spear," I whispered. "But we have to get out of here."

"You do? Where was it?" Simone didn't sound as excited as I thought she would.

"Her grandmother gave it to her," Asher said with an edge to his voice.

"She had it all along?" Simone asked. "The Knights were letting people get killed even though they had it?"

"Yes, well . . . no. It's complicated. She had to keep it a secret from everyone." I didn't like lying—I wasn't good at it. "We can talk about this later, after we get out of here."

Asher stared at me, not saying a word.

"But why keep it a secret if innocent people were being killed? It doesn't make sense." Simone sounded skeptical.

"Maybe she's been lying to us . . . about everything. The spear might even be a fake. Something to get rid of us."

I couldn't tell her that I knew it was the real one because I had just used it to save my father and change destiny. My story and lies were starting to unravel.

"It's not a fake," I said. "She's been waiting to give it to me for years." I glanced around, nervous that someone might have seen me dig up the spear. "But can we just get out of here before we get caught?"

"Well, first let me see it." Simone held out her hand.

"Why? You wouldn't know if it's real even if you saw it," Asher answered.

"No, but I assume you would," Simone retorted. "Have *you* checked it out?"

Asher squirmed at the realization that he hadn't even confirmed if I'd been given the real spear. He opened my bag and looked inside. "It looks authentic, but only Zio would know for sure." He still had his jaw clenched, but his shoulders had relaxed a little. "And you're sure you never touched it?"

"I already told you that I didn't," I said, glancing at Simone. "I don't want to be bound."

"Okay." Asher seemed to finally buy my story. "But I'm keeping the bag from now on," he said, shoving it into his backpack. "I don't want you even close to it."

"Fine. Let's just get back to the monastery. The sooner we get there, the sooner everything can go back to how it was before."

"Yeah, just like before," Simone muttered, but her voice had a hint of sadness in it.

I crossed the garden into another small courtyard. We had to go before anyone tried to stop us.

"So we just walk out with it?" Simone asked, following close behind.

"Why not? We're not prisoners." The main gate was up ahead.

In the quiet of the night, we heard a door closing. We all turned around to see Massimo walking out of the building. He spotted us and broke into a run. I could hear his heavy footsteps pounding the ground. "Stop! Where are you going?" he shouted. "You need to stay here!"

"*Don't* stop," Asher said under his breath. "Keep going."

We picked up the pace, but Massimo intercepted us as I reached the locked gate.

"You can't leave," Massimo said, blocking the door. "Dame Elisabeth did not approve of this."

"We'll come back another day," I said. "But we need to go. It's getting very late."

Massimo hesitated, unsure of what to do.

Asher took a step forward, getting between Massimo and me.

"Open the gate," Asher ordered, his voice deep and strong.

Massimo glared at him.

"Open it," Asher repeated.

This time Massimo turned and unlocked the door.

Asher, Simone, and I exchanged quick glances. This hadn't been as difficult as we'd thought. Soon all this would be over.

We had only taken a few steps out of the compound when Massimo suddenly grabbed me by the arm and yanked me back next to him. The tip of his gun jabbed me in the ribs.

Asher and Simone both spun around to face us.

"Neither of you moves," Massimo sneered, "or she dies."

—TWENTY-FIVE—

You'd think I would have been more afraid of having a gun pressed against my side, but the events of the last two days had substantially increased my tolerance for fear. I didn't go weak in the knees nor did my heart race. In fact, it seemed that my breathing slowed down as I tried to think of a way to escape.

Asher and Simone, however, were another story. They weren't moving, but I could see the shock and panic in their eyes.

"Why are you doing this?" I tried to buy some time while I glanced around the empty courtyard. The area was enclosed by the large cement wall, and the only way out was the street we had come in by. "Aren't you a Knight?"

Massimo scoffed. "You'd think after working security for them for over ten years they'd make me one, but no." His breath hit the side of my ear as he talked. "Dame Elisabeth kept promising, but it was all a lie to string me along. It's time I took care of myself." He pushed me forward, holding me in front of him like a shield. "Now walk to that first alleyway."

"I can pay you a lot of money if you let her go," Simone blurted out while we walked past her.

"Ha!" Massimo kept walking with me. "As if you could match what the Hastati will give me for a marked one. Now you two better not come any closer."

I looked at Asher. He was standing still, his fists clenched. Maybe my chance at escape was farther down the street.

"You don't understand. I can give you as much as you want!" Simone shouted. "My mother is Sarah Bimington!"

Massimo paused, apparently considering Simone's offer.

"You know they'll kill me if you turn me in," I said, trying to make him feel guilty for what he was doing.

"That isn't my problem." He shook his head. "No, I'm taking you to the Hastati. You can bargain for your life with them." He tightened his grip on my arm, pushed the gun harder into my ribs, and led me to the first alleyway. "Try anything funny and I will shoot you. My understanding is that there is still money to be made even if you are dead."

"Massimo! Massimo!" I could hear Dame Elisabeth calling him in the distance.

"Walk faster," he ordered as we stepped into the alley. "To that green car."

There were no doors or open windows along the buildings that framed either side of the dimly lit alley. The only escape route seemed to be about a block down, where the alley opened up at a busy street.

I was out of time.

If I got into the dusty old car, my chances of escape would go from slim to none. I had to make my move.

As we approached the green car, Massimo loosened his grip on my arm for a second to fish out his keys. It was a split-second decision, but I made it. This was my last chance.

I spun away, hoping to catch him by surprise. Darting between two parked cars, I started running toward the street. I was about halfway there when I heard a bang and felt a bullet whizz by my head.

I froze.

"Next one won't miss," Massimo shouted.

This time I was scared. Wet-my-pants, cold-shiver-down-my-spine, nothing-can-really-prepare-you scared. I raised my hands and slowly turned to face him.

He had a smirk on his face, but only for an instant. Something behind me caught his attention, and as if in slow motion, I saw him pull the trigger.

I held my breath, expecting the bullet to hit.

Only it didn't. I wasn't his target.

And in that moment the sound of gunfire came from both in front and behind.

Massimo staggered and fell to the ground.

I spun around to see Dame Elisabeth walking up the alley, a gun in her hand.

"Get out of here, Cassandra!" She kept her gun aimed at Massimo. "Now!"

I took off, not waiting to see what else was going to happen between Dame Elisabeth and Massimo.

"Come on!" Simone yelled. She and Asher were by the street corner.

"Go!" I said, already sprinting at full speed. "GO!"

We didn't stop running until we were back at the metro station.

"How . . . how . . ." I bent over to catch my breath. "How did she know to save me?" I asked, trying to piece together everything that had happened.

Simone was in no condition to talk. She was leaning against the ticket machine and her breathing was coming in and out in short, quick spurts.

Asher was the only one who didn't look wiped out. He bought our metro passes from the machine and took one deep breath to regain his composure. "It was Simone," he said. "She ran back into the compound and found your grandmother, running out. The security camera by the front gate had captured Massimo grabbing you. Simone told her what happened."

I put a hand on Simone's back. "Thanks. You saved my butt."

Simone gave me a small nod and sat down. She was still having trouble breathing.

"We should head to the monastery," Asher said, checking the time on his phone. "We can be there in about thirty minutes."

I nodded. I'd nearly been shot, but now it was all almost over. I had the spear, my dad was awake, and he'd be leaving whatever hospital he was in by tomorrow morning. All that was left was to give Brother Gregorio the spear and everything would fall into place—just like I'd seen in my vision.

What could go wrong?

—TWENTY-SIX—

Streetlights cast long shadows around every corner as we neared the monastery. None of us said anything, but I knew we were all on edge.

"I don't think this is a good idea. What if the Hastati have someone waiting for us outside the building?" Simone slowed down. "We could be heading into a trap. Maybe we should go to my house."

I wasn't going to quit when I was so close to getting my dad and my life back. "We'll be careful, but we have to get the spear to Brother Gregorio. It's the only way."

"No, Simone's right," Asher said. "They probably are watching all the doors to the monastery. That's why we're not going in that way." Asher stopped walking and pointed to a dimly lit curio shop. "Follow me."

Inside, we made our way past a middle-aged bearded man sitting behind a cash register. He gave us a slight nod as Asher placed a twenty-euro bill on the counter and we continued toward the rear of the store.

"Where are we going?" I asked. We weaved our way around stacks of books, a table full of brass knickknacks, and a glass cabinet with more ceramic cat figurines than I'd ever seen.

Asher pointed to a room, partially hidden by a faded green curtain.

He pushed open the curtain and motioned for us to enter. "There's a secret passage . . . here." He peeled away a small rug to reveal a trapdoor. "Rome is full of them. It's like the city was built on top of an old maze. You'd be surprised at how many—"

"We know all about it." Simone cut him off. "I have one at my place, too."

"Oh . . . well, yeah. It's just I don't think many people know about this one. Not even Zio."

We followed Asher into a pit under the curio shop. There were a few storage boxes, but not much else. No tunnels or passageways.

"Now what?" I asked, looking around.

"Now we crawl." Asher smiled and removed a small metal grille that covered an opening near the base of the far wall.

The space was definitely not made for anyone claustro-phobic, but it was a safe way to get into the monastery and that was all that mattered.

"Are we there yet?" Simone called out from behind.

"Almost." Asher reached another metal grille and unscrewed two knobs at the top. He pushed it aside and crawled out. Reaching above his head, he pulled on a cord and turned on a single lightbulb that hung in the middle of the room. "Ta-da! I present Zio's wine cellar."

The rock walls around us were lined with dark wooden racks. A few of them had bottles, but most were empty and full of dust.

"We're in the monastery?" Simone slapped off the dirt from her pants and hands.

"Yep." Asher smiled and walked over to a rickety old staircase. "Zio can't make it down these stairs, so I'm the one who has to get the bottles of wine for him. One day I started moving some of these shelves and found the crawl space. Decided to see where it would lead. It's been my secret way out for a while now."

"Hmpf." Simone shrugged. "I guess you're not as lame as I thought you were."

I should've felt relief at being inside the monastery, but for some reason I didn't. I knew we were supposed to be safe once inside, but I couldn't relax. "And the guy at the shop doesn't ask any questions? Just lets you come and go?"

"I usually bring him something," Asher explained. "A bottle of wine or some cash. I think of it as a toll."

"Okay, whatever." Simone walked to the stairs. "Can we just take the spear to your uncle and be finished with all of this?"

Simone was right. It was almost over.

A small, secretive grin swept across my face. I'd done it. I had actually found the spear, changed destiny, and saved my dad. It wasn't something I could ever share with anyone, but it made me feel powerful, like I could do anything. The best thing was that by tomorrow morning, at 11:58 a.m., during a huge thunderstorm, I'd be with my father. All I had to do was get Brother Gregorio to tell me where he was being kept.

Asher bounded up the stairs, taking the steps three at a time. He reached into his backpack and pulled out a key to unlock the door at the top. "After you," he said, holding it open for Simone and me.

The moment I stepped into the kitchen, I knew something was wrong. Through the French doors I could see that all the lights in the monastery were off, and it seemed eerily quiet.

"Zio, are you here?" Asher called out, flicking the kitchen light on.

Silence.

We wandered out of the kitchen into the dining room, and then into the dark courtyard.

The hairs on the back of my neck stood up. "Is he here?" I asked in a whisper.

"Maybe he went out," Simone suggested. The three of us walked together as one huddled mass.

Asher opened his switchblade. He lifted his hand and motioned for us to stay put. Like a ninja slipping in and out of the shadows, he made his way to the old monk's office.

Simone and I stayed near the front door. A trickle of sweat ran down my side as we saw the light in the monk's office turn on.

"Zio!" Asher yelled, and I could hear the shock and fear in his voice.

Simone and I looked at each other, but instead of running away we raced toward Asher. We froze once we got to the room. There, in his leather chair, was Brother Gregorio. His head was thrown back, his skin was pale, and his eyes, although wide open, weren't seeing anything. Asher was kneeling next to him holding his uncle's limp hand.

"Is he . . . ?" Simone couldn't finish the sentence.

Asher's eyes met mine, and he gave a slight shake of his head. Brother Gregorio was dead.

The key to finding my dad, to stopping the Hastati, was gone.

"We have to get out of here!" Simone exclaimed. "Whoever did this could still be here!"

"No one did this." Asher stood and closed his uncle's eyelids. "Zio told me weeks ago that he only had a short time to live. Even last night he warned me that I might be on my own very soon."

I scanned the room. There was no sign of a struggle; everything looked like the organized mess I'd seen the day before. But what if Asher was wrong and there was something more sinister at work?

"I can call my mother. She'll help us," Simone offered.

"No!" Asher barked. "It's bad enough that you're involved. We're not telling more people!"

I realized that as upset as I was at losing the key to finding my dad, Asher had just lost his only family. "Asher." I reached over and touched his shoulder. "Simone is only trying to help. She didn't mean anything bad by it."

"I know, I know." He pushed my hand away. "I have to stay focused." He took a deep breath, slowly letting it out. "Zio taught me to put my feelings aside. I have a job to do."

"I am sorry about your uncle," Simone said.

Asher bent over and gave the old monk a small kiss on the forehead. "You've prepared me well, Zio," Asher whispered. "I can do this. It'll be fine."

Simone and I stayed quiet until Asher was ready to face us.

"I need to get something," he said, sidestepping me and walking out of the room. "My uncle had a plan," he called out. "For whenever this happened. Someone I was supposed to call."

Across the courtyard in the living room, Asher went straight to a small desk and opened the top two drawers. He rifled through them. "The number is here . . . somewhere." He pointed around the room. "Look for a small red book. It has instructions in it."

"But who are you calling?" I asked as Asher continued to search a nearby bookcase. "Can we trust him?"

Asher froze, then looked at me. "Uh, well, I don't know. I'm not even sure who he is."

"Seriously," Simone whispered to me, "isn't my mother a better option?"

"No, she's not," Asher answered her. His voice had a threatening edge to it. "My uncle's orders were that no one else find out about this, and it's my duty to make sure that no one does. Got it?"

"Fine." Simone raised her hands in surrender. "But shouldn't we at least get out of here? Go somewhere else?"

"The monastery is supposed to be the safest place, remember?" I paced around the room.

"Wait." Simone backed away from me. "You expect us to stay here with . . . with a . . ." She lowered her voice. "A dead body?"

"No. Well, yeah," I said. "But just for tonight. And shhh—that's Asher's uncle."

"Found it!" Asher pulled out a red address book from beneath a folder. He flipped through it, then stopped to look at me. "Cassie, I know we don't know this guy, but my uncle trusted him—"

"No way. Uh-uh." I shook my head. "I'm not going on the run again in the middle of the night if it turns out that this person isn't one of the good guys."

"The monastery isn't safe anymore. My uncle was the one guaranteeing us protection from the Hastati—with him gone, there's no agreement. Nothing to stop them from coming in here and taking you."

"See," Simone said. "We should go."

"But no one even knows we've snuck back in here," I argued while trying to reason everything out. "This is the safest place—at least for tonight."

Asher thought about it for a few seconds, then tossed the book on the desk. "Fine, for one night."

Simone gave me a very hesitant nod. "One night."

"Deal," I said, knowing that one night was all I needed because I'd already seen tomorrow, and it was going to be everything I'd wished for.

—TWENTY-SEVEN—

Once we were back in our bedroom, Simone and I collapsed onto the bed. The rush of adrenaline from the entire day had been replaced by total exhaustion. Within minutes, we were both asleep.

Not that I rested much. I kept having nightmares that jarred me awake. I'd dream of dead and decaying bodies littering the sidewalks and camouflaged military trucks patrolling the streets. There were people chasing me until I was cornered on the edge of a rooftop and lost my balance. Plunging to my certain death, I'd wake up. After the fourth time this happened, I decided to go do something productive—find out what instructions Brother Gregorio had left for Asher in that red book.

I tiptoed around the dark room, making sure not to wake up Simone. Taking the unused burner phone off the night table to use its flashlight feature, I noticed an unread text message.

Simone, tell me where you are. You have to trust me. I'm your mother—I know what's best.

I stared at the message, wondering how Simone's mother could know this number. It was supposed to be an untraceable throwaway cell. I searched the call history and saw it: A call had been made the day before while we were in Orvieto.

Even though she knew that we weren't supposed to use the phones, she had called her mother anyway. I wanted to shake her out of her peaceful sleep. She could've given away our location and put us all in danger. How could she be so stupid and selfish? I took out the phone's battery and tossed both pieces on the bed.

"No . . . I can't," Simone mumbled, then turned over . . . still asleep.

Every trace of anger evaporated. I couldn't forget that she was putting herself at risk because of me. She had probably been freaked out after being held hostage by the half-eared man and had wanted to talk to her mom. We just had to be more careful. I would talk to her about it in the morning.

Once in the breezeway, I could see the courtyard down below, bathed in a soft glow as dawn broke and the morning's first light filtered through the skylight above.

The monastery was quiet and peaceful. I glanced over at the closed door of Brother Gregorio's office. There might be information in there, but I couldn't find the courage to go inside while Brother Gregorio's body was still in that chair. The red book would have to do for now. Entering the living room, I noticed we had left all the lights on the night before and that the book was right where Asher had left it—on the desk. I picked it up and began thumbing through it when Asher bolted up from the couch behind me, a knife in his hands.

It was so unexpected that I let out a small scream and dropped the book, knocking down a folder that was on the desk in the process.

"Who? What?" Asher waved the kitchen knife in front of him, his eyes still not focusing on me.

"It's me," I said, catching my breath. "Didn't mean to startle you."

"Oh." Asher plopped back down on the couch. "I must've dozed off."

I noticed the dark circles under his eyes. "Have you been down here all night?"

"Yeah." He put the knife on the coffee table in front of him. "I couldn't sleep. Plus, I had some stuff to think about."

"And the knife?" I asked.

"Protection." He yawned. "In case anybody tried to get to you. What are you doing down here so early?"

"Couldn't sleep, either." I bent down to pick up the book and a couple of papers that had slipped out of the folder. "Figured I could use the time to learn a little bit more about what's going on."

"From the instructions Zio left me?"

"You never know. There could be . . ." One of the papers on the floor caught my eye, and I stopped talking. It was a grainy black-and-white still shot from a security camera that showed two men pushing a stretcher into a building.

I put everything else back on the desk and studied the photograph. A date stamp on the bottom left showed that it was taken the day all of this had started.

My hand started to tremble. *Could it be?* It was hard to be sure, but the patient looked like my dad and the place could definitely be the one I'd seen in my vision. It had to be him.

"Asher, check this out." I showed him the photograph. There was a name over the front doors—Casa di Cura Oreste. "Do you know this place?"

Asher studied it for a few seconds, and then shook his head. "No, but is that your dad?"

Excitement bubbled up in my chest. My father was going to be released from this place today, this very morning, and now I could be there when he got out. I was bouncing on my toes, anxious to leave and find my dad. "I have to get there before noon. We have to find this place. Where's your laptop?"

"You had it last, remember? And why before noon?" Asher was barely reacting to our discovery. Then again, it wasn't his father we were saving. He didn't even know my dad.

"I . . . um . . . I just . . ." My thoughts were flying off in all directions, and I couldn't think of what to say.

Asher held up his hand. "Before you lie to me again, you should know that I already figured out what you did."

"I didn't do anything," I said, inching away from him.

"You did. I went along with your story about your grandmother putting the spear in your bag because I didn't want to believe you'd actually use the spear, but deep inside I knew you had."

I stayed quiet.

Asher grabbed me by the shoulders. "Listen, Cassie. I'm not mad, but don't keep lying about it. My uncle's death confirmed it for me." He stared into my eyes. "I'm okay with being bound along with you—it's what I was born to do—but you should've told me."

"Wait, what?" I pushed away his hand. "What do you mean you're bound? I thought you didn't have the mark."

"No, not bound to the spear. Bound to you."

"Me?" I had no idea what he was talking about. How could I have bound him? I'd thought only marked ones became bound to the spear. The confusion on my face must have been obvious, because Asher started shaking his head.

"Don't you know what happened? Back in the garden," he said. "I thought my uncle had explained everything to you."

I stayed quiet.

"Did he even tell you about Tobias? The person that was bound to the spear before you."

"Yeah, a little bit, but like I already said, I'm not bound to—"

"To the spear. Yeah, I got it." He paced around the room for a moment. "So you know Tobias had some crazy plan for making the world a better place by basically killing off most of the population, right?"

I nodded.

"Did my uncle mention he was Tobias's Guardian?"

"You mean instead of his parents?" I wasn't sure how that affected anything except for the fact that Brother Gregorio was Asher's guardian, too.

"No, not like a legal guardian. Guardian in the Hastati sense of the word." He paused to watch my reaction. Seeing none, he continued. "Do you know what the Guardian does?"

"Don't they control the spear? It's the person with a birthmark who guards the spear, and if they become bound to it then they can change destiny. Like me . . . if I were to be bound to it, which I'm not."

"Oh, wow." Asher ran his hands through his hair and looked at me incredulously. "I can't believe you've been running around without knowing all the facts." He shook his head. "You really don't know, do you?" he asked. "Cassie, you aren't the Guardian . . . I am!"

None of what he was saying made sense. How could he be the Guardian? Wasn't the Guardian bound to the spear?

Asher took me by the hand and sat me on the couch next to him. "Okay, I don't know why Zio didn't tell you everything, but here it is. The spear is made up of two things, the actual spearhead and the marked person that's bound to it. You need both to access the power to change destiny. Make sense so far?"

"Yeah, I kinda knew that already."

"Okay, so a bound person is necessary to use the spear and that makes this person a huge target for the Hastati. I mean, obviously we've seen that people will be hunted down and killed just because they have the mark and the potential of being part of the spear's power. But the Guardian is someone who protects the person who is bound to the spear . . .

makes sure no one harms them in this world and that they don't get lost inside the Realm of Possibilities."

A shiver ran down my spine at the thought of what could have happened when I used the spear to save my dad. That giant void I'd felt and the visions I'd seen must be what he was talking about. "What exactly is it? The realm . . . ?"

"I don't know much about it," Asher admitted. "It's like another dimension or something. People who go inside can get lost in it if a Guardian doesn't ground them to reality. That's why every bound person basically gets a Guardian . . . for life."

I clasped my neck and pulled my head back. This was a lot to absorb.

"It gets weirder," Asher warned. "When I say for life, it's really 'for life.' The Guardian will die if something happens to the marked person that's bound to the spear. It's like a built-in incentive to do a good job and not turn on them."

"And what makes you think you're my Guardian?" I asked.

"Didn't you feel it? In the garden when I touched you. I tried convincing myself that it was just some weird static electricity, but it wasn't." He sighed. "Then when we found my uncle, I knew for sure."

"I don't see what your uncle has to do with it," I said, still very confused.

"My uncle was Tobias's Guardian; it was his job to protect him. But he knew that Tobias wasn't going to live much longer, which meant he would die soon, too."

"So Tobias is dead?"

"Probably. I mean, a Guardian's death doesn't really affect the person who's bound to the spear . . . But chances are my uncle died because Tobias died."

"Ok-a-a-a-y."

"Which means that the spear's power was up for grabs again. So *someone*"—Asher raised his eyebrows and stressed the word—"could become bound and use the spear."

"Uh-huh."

"And that *someone* would need a Guardian to bring them out of the realm."

I swallowed the lump in my throat. It wasn't only my life that was forever changed by the spear; I had changed Asher's, too. Now I felt guilty.

"I . . . I didn't know I was bringing you into it," I stammered.

"Aha!" He pointed a finger at me. "You admit you touched it!"

"What! You made all that up?"

"No, no. Everything I said is true. I just wanted you to finally admit it!" He sat back against the sofa. "So now that I'm forever involved, are you going to tell me what you did and why we have to find your dad before noon?"

I hesitated. I'd convinced myself that no one would ever know what I'd done, that being bound wouldn't change anything as long as I never used the spear again and just turned it over to the Hastati. But this was now a secret I'd have to share with Asher.

"I used it to save my dad. He was dying; I saw it!" I took a breath. "So I changed the future. Picked a path where he was alive and I even saw that I'd be with him at the hospital today at 11:58 in the morning. I had no choice. I couldn't let him die."

Asher simply nodded. I couldn't forget that he'd lost both his parents and now his uncle. Maybe he would've done the same thing for them if given a chance.

"That's what I figured," he said.

"I was willing to sacrifice myself for my dad, but I didn't mean for anything to happen to you. Maybe if I'd known, I—"

"An early morning rendezvous?" Simone called out. She had one hand on the doorframe and a smug look on her face. Her smirk quickly faded as she realized that she'd just interrupted a serious conversation. "What's going on?"

"Nothing," Asher responded, his left foot pushing against mine. "Nothing at all."

Simone drew closer. "Cassie, what's going on?"

She knew something was up, but I couldn't tell her what I'd done. It was bad enough that I'd managed to suck Asher into all of this; I couldn't do that to Simone. It wouldn't be fair to her.

"My dad," I said. "I think we know where he is." I got up and took the picture from the desk to show her. "I think it's a hospital or something."

"Casa di Cura Oreste," Simone read the name out loud. "Are we going there? Is that what you were talking about?"

Asher and I exchanged a brief look. "Yes," we both said in unison.

"Uh-huh." Simone didn't look convinced. "And once we go there and get your dad, then what?"

"We give the spear to the Hastati and then everything goes back to normal," I said.

"Cassie, I hate to break it to you, but the Hastati aren't going to just let you go. And where are you going to go that they won't find you? Even with fake passports." Simone was pointing out some big holes in my plan. "I think we need to make sure we have some leverage, something that leaves the Hastati with no choice but to back off."

"Like what?" We had no leverage except the spear. Was she thinking that we should hold it hostage or hide it again? But that would just make us even bigger targets.

"I don't know." Simone looked away. "Something."

"I think we should call the guy my uncle mentioned." Asher stood up to get the red book. "He might be able to help."

"Or he might not," I pointed out. "Why don't we wait and see what my dad says, okay?"

"But your dad might not be in any condition to help us." Simone bit the edge of her fingernail. "He was in a coma."

I wanted so badly to tell her that everything was going to be fine. It was killing me to have her worry needlessly. "I have a feeling he'll be okay. So let's find him first and then we can decide, all right?"

"I still think we need help," Simone said under her breath.

I gave Asher a look, pleading with my eyes for him to back me up.

"Cassie's right." Asher gave me a slight nod. "Let's see what we find before we get anyone else involved." He stood up and went to the door. "I'll go get my laptop so we can figure out how to get to Casa di Cura Oreste."

"Guess I'm outnumbered." Simone shrugged and focused on her nail again. "We'll do it your way."

I thought she had decided to go along with our idea, but the moment Asher was gone, Simone pulled me off the couch and dragged me to the far corner of the room. "Listen, before Asher gets back," she whispered, "we should really talk about contacting my mom. We—you, your dad, and me—can all go to my house in Praiano. It's like a fortress. No one will find us. Once we're there my mom can help us figure out who should get the spear."

"Simone, no." I couldn't be more definitive in my answer. "You haven't told her anything, have you?"

"Of course not."

"*Simo-o-ne?*" My eyes narrowed, and I tried reading her. "I know you called your mother when we were in Orvieto."

Simone's jaw dropped. "How did you find out?"

"I saw it on the phone's call history." I reached for her hand. "Don't worry, I get it. You were freaked out after the half-eared guy grabbed you, but you promised me that you wouldn't say anything. If the Hastati find out we've told someone, they might take it out on my dad."

"Cassie, I'd never do anything that would hurt you or your dad." She wrapped her arms around me and squeezed. "You have to believe me."

And since she was my best friend, I did.

—TWENTY-EIGHT—

During the next hour we discovered that the place where my dad was being kept was about thirty minutes outside of Rome and that it was more of a convalescent clinic where long-term patients were treated. We couldn't find many pictures or descriptions of the layout of the building, only the same standard picture from the front. But even from that shot, you could tell the building was somewhat remote, with nothing around it. There were also no trains or buses that went there, either, which meant we had to get a car.

The three of us were sitting around a small kitchen table trying to figure out our next move.

"What if we ask Gisak?" Asher suggested. "My friend from the curio shop. He'd probably close the shop for the day and do it if I gave him two hundred euros."

"Great friend." Simone rolled her eyes. "You have to pay him for a favor."

"Better than hiring a driver who turns out to be a killer," Asher retorted. "I think it's our best bet."

"Fine." I took a sip of some orange juice. "But do you think he'll do it with no questions asked?"

"Yeah." Asher smiled. "We have an understanding. I've done him some questionable favors in the past in exchange for him letting me sneak in and out of the monastery. I don't think he'll want to know what we are doing."

"Questionable?" Simone raised an eyebrow. I had to admit, I was intrigued, too.

"Let's just say he doesn't always get everything in his shop in the most legit way." Seeing our expressions, he immediately backtracked. "No, no, I don't steal stuff or anything. He's just had me follow some unsavory people. Report back to him before he deals with them."

"Oh." There was a lot about Asher that I didn't know.

"The only catch is that he probably won't get there until closer to nine. We'll have to wait."

"Then let's go wait for him there . . . in case we get lucky and he shows up early," I said.

"Lucky," Simone scoffed. "Because we've been *so-o-o* lucky this far. This is getting ridiculous."

"Hey, we found the spear and Cassie's dad; that's pretty good," Asher said a little defensively.

"Uh-huh, but your uncle also died," she answered flatly.

"Simone!" I couldn't believe she'd said that. Asher had lost his only family and had accepted being bound to me, *for life*, as if it were no big deal. How could she be so mean?

"Sorry," she said. "But I don't think either one of you is looking at the reality of what's happening. Things are messed up and they aren't getting much better."

This was not the Simone I was used to seeing. It was like something had changed inside her.

"Things will get better." Asher glanced over at me. "I believe in Cassie."

"Well isn't that special," Simone said in a sarcastic tone. "I do, too, but that's not what I'm talking about." She shook her head and sighed. "Never mind." She pushed her chair away and headed out of the kitchen.

"She doesn't understand," I said. "Once we get to my dad, she'll be fine. She's just worried."

"Honestly, I don't care."

By nine o'clock we had crawled back through the tunnel and were sitting on small, three-legged leather stools in the back room of the curio shop waiting for Gisak. The smell of incense permeated every corner of the shop, and it felt like we were all meditating as we sat in silence. Finally, the bells hanging by the front door tinkled as Gisak entered the store.

Asher jumped up. "Stay here. I'll be right back."

True to what Asher expected, Gisak agreed to take us to the clinic. He put a CLOSED sign on the door and went to get his car without even taking a second look at us.

As we waited outside for Gisak to bring the car, I glanced around the street. It was still relatively early, and not many people were out and about. I took a deep breath, inhaling the cool morning air before wiping my sweaty palms on my jeans.

I hadn't told Asher everything about my vision. I'd left out the part about the shooting, the people in the hazmat suits, and the dead bodies in the street. If that was part of the future, I might have to use the spear one more time to change it. Except this time, I'd have to learn how to navigate inside the Realm and make sure Asher was able to pull me out. I stole a look at Asher's profile. We'd make a good team. We had to; there was no other choice.

A beat-up blue car that looked like it should be headed to a junkyard and not a highway pulled up. Gisak leaned across a seat that was covered in duct tape and unlocked the door.

"Sorry, door doesn't open from the outside," he said as we all got in.

I glanced at the car's clock. It was 9:44. In a little over two hours I'd be with my dad at the clinic.

"So what's the plan?" Simone asked from the backseat. "Should we call and find out what room he's in? I can disguise my voice."

That caught Gisak's attention, and I saw him do a quick check on us in the rearview mirror.

"No, don't do that." Asher shook his head. "We don't want to tip them off."

He had a good point. We couldn't let them know we were coming. "We'll just have to search for him when we get there."

"Him who?" Gisak asked, then waved his hands in the air. "Never mind. I don't want to know."

Realizing that everything we said was being shared with Gisak, we all shut up.

Twenty-five minutes later, we were pulling into a long driveway that led to what could have easily passed for an average, nondescript apartment complex. Nothing about the place looked like a medical facility, and I would've thought we'd made a mistake if it weren't for the fact that above the front doors were the words *Casa di Cura Oreste*.

Gisak parked the car in one of the visitor spaces and turned to Asher. "I told you before that I don't want to know what you're doing, but I can tell you're into something serious. You need to be careful."

"I have it under control. You know I'm resourceful." Asher gave him a smirk before turning to us. "We just need to make sure that they don't notice us or question our being there."

As he said this, a young woman exited the building and we could all see a security guard sitting behind a desk.

"That guard will definitely stop us," Simone observed.

I took in the surroundings. There were several delivery trucks on the far side of the clinic, including one for a florist.

I glanced at Asher. With his dark hair and his perfect Italian, he could pass for a local. "Okay, I have an idea. You see that florist van?" I pointed to the white van with red roses painted on the side that was parked between two large delivery trucks. "Asher, can you grab a few bouquets so we can pretend to be delivering them to the post-op nurses?"

Gisak stroked his beard but said nothing, although he was listening intently.

"And I'm supposed to just take the flowers?" Asher asked. "You don't think someone's going to try to stop me?"

"That's where Simone and I come in. We'll distract the delivery guys and meet you in the front lobby."

Simone was shaking her head. She didn't like the plan. "That's not going to work. How are we going to distract them long enough for Asher to steal the flowers?"

"It will work," I insisted. "We just need a diversion . . . a good one." I looked around, trying to come up with something. "That dumpster over by the last truck. We can start a small fire in it and call for help. When everyone runs over, Asher grabs the flowers."

"I think we should be the ones grabbing the flowers," Simone argued. "No reason we should risk being labeled arsonists."

"That's really the least of my problems right now," I answered. "But maybe you should stay with Gisak in the car. Honk the horn if you see something going wrong and make sure Gisak doesn't leave us if we get caught." I glanced at our driver and new coconspirator. "No offense."

"None taken," he said. "And the plan . . . it could work," Gisak added, nodding his head in approval.

"Fine," Simone relented. "So how do you plan on starting this blaze?"

"I don't have matches or a lighter in the bag," Asher replied before I could even ask.

Gisak held up a silver lighter. "I use this for the incense." He pushed a button to pop open the trunk. "And there might be a flare in the car kit back there if you want more smoke than fire."

I eyed him suspiciously. He didn't seem to be the type of person who would volunteer to help for the sake of being nice. "Why are you doing this?" I asked. "You don't even know us . . . and it's not just for a couple hundred euros."

"Asher, he's a good kid, and you are his friends." He paused. "And in my business, it's important to be able to judge the value of things. One day, I may ask for a favor in return."

His words seemed to linger in the air. I took the lighter from his outstretched hand as a few raindrops fell on the windshield. I knew from my vision that the thunder and lightning weren't far behind. "Okay," I said and opened the door.

"I hope you know what you're doing, Cassie," Simone said as I got out of the car.

I smiled and gave her a wink. "I absolutely do."

—TWENTY-NINE—

Standing behind the dumpster, I glanced around one more time to make sure the coast was clear. Simone was waiting in Gisak's car, and Asher was hiding behind a van, ready to steal the flowers. It all depended on me now.

I pulled out the lighter and flare that I'd tucked inside my leather jacket. The instructions on the side of the stick seemed simple enough. Take the top part off and strike the base like you would a match. If that didn't work then I'd just use the lighter.

On the first try, a cascade of sparks came flying off like a Fourth-of-July sparkler, and the stick burned brightly. Quickly, I tossed it into the dumpster. Within a few seconds smoke started coming out. It was time. I ran behind a nearby column.

"Fuoco, fuoco!" Simone shouted, stepping out of Gisak's car and pointing to the dumpster.

A nearby deliveryman looked over, saw the smoke, and began calling for help. Everyone in the area ran toward the dumpster.

I raced over to the front entrance, where Simone and Asher were already waiting. They each had flower baskets filled with daisies and white roses that Asher had grabbed while I caused the distraction. Simone handed me one, but her eyes kept scanning the area.

"Something wrong?" I whispered as the dark clouds began to roll in. The storm was coming . . . just like in my vision.

Simone shook her head. "Just making sure no one is here to kill us."

Once we got inside, our flower delivery wasn't questioned. We said we were delivering a set of flowers to the nurses' stations on each floor. The guard handed us visitor passes and pointed to the elevator down the hall.

Stepping into the elevator I let out a long, shaky breath. I was jumble of excitement and nerves. My dad was here. I could feel it. We'd be leaving with him soon.

"Which floor do we start on?" Simone asked, her finger hovering over the elevator buttons.

"Let's start at the top." I reached over and pushed the number five.

We exited on the fifth floor and peered into every room before dropping off a bouquet of flowers with the nurses. We did the same on the fourth, and there was still no sign of my dad.

"What if he's not awake?" Simone whispered as we dropped off the second bouquet. "If he's still in a coma. Would you at least think of talking to my mom? I really think she can help."

"I don't know," I muttered, not wanting to accept that as a possibility. "He'll be awake, you'll see."

Splitting up on the third floor, we each darted toward a different room along the hospital's wide hallway. The nurses' station was on the far end, away from the elevator, so like the other floors, we could pop into the rooms without drawing too much attention.

The first two rooms I checked were empty, but the third had a frail old man hooked to an IV, with an oxygen tube in his nose. There was such sadness in his eyes, but it seemed to lessen when he saw the flowers in my hand.

"*Scuzi*, I have the wrong room," I said, but I could tell that he didn't understand English. He motioned for me to put the flowers on the table by his bed.

"*Grazie*," he whispered, a slight smile filtering over his face.

I set down the bouquet, allowing him to think that someone had sent them for him. *Could Simone be right? What if my father was like this old man? I wouldn't be able to just unplug him. No*, I thought, *he'll be fine. He has to be.*

"Cassie!" Simone was calling me. "I found him."

My heart pounded as I ran out of the old man's room. I paused and looked up and down the hallway, unsure of where to go.

"Over here," Simone said from the room next door.

I ran over only to be confronted by Simone standing rigidly by the window, a pained look on her face.

The rhythmic beeping of a machine filled the room.

My eyes immediately darted toward the hospital bed. My father was there, but he was unconscious and his body was hooked up to monitors.

I rushed over and picked up his hand. It felt warm, but it was limp.

No! This isn't how it's supposed to be! I glanced up at the clock above his bed. It was 10:52, which, according to my vision, meant that my father was supposed to be talking to me in about an hour. *Was I supposed to just wait here?*

"Papi, wake up," I pleaded. "You have to wake up. *¡Despiértate!* We don't have much time."

"I'm sorry, Cassie," Simone said, staring at her feet. "I had to do it."

"Do it?" Asher repeated, taking a few steps into the room. Behind him the door closed and my blood ran cold as I heard the click of a gun.

—THIRTY—

"Step away from the bed," a deep voice instructed. "And go stand next to your friend."

Out of the corner of my eye, I could tell it was the half-eared man. I slowly turned to face him.

He waved the gun toward Asher. "You get over there, too."

The sound of someone laughing outside in the hallway caught everyone's attention, and in the split second that the half-eared man was distracted, Asher made his move—lunging at him.

The half-eared man quickly lifted up his hand and pistol-whipped Asher across the side of the jaw, knocking him out cold.

"Asher!" I crouched down next to him, trying to protect him from the assassin.

"Shh! Not another word." The half-eared man pushed me away from Asher, his gun in my face. "Scream and I will shoot him, understand?"

I nodded.

"Good. Now move over to the window."

I rose and took the remaining steps backward, my eyes not leaving Asher, until I bumped into the wall.

"I'm so sorry," Simone muttered again.

"It's not your fault." I reached over and gripped her hand. "You had to call us. He had a gun on you."

"Tie his wrists around the bed." The gunman reached into his pocket and tossed a zip-tie to Simone. "I don't want to take any more chances."

Simone did as she was told, pulling Asher's right arm around the bedpost and then tying his two wrists together with the plastic tie. Just as she finished, the half-eared man threw her another zip-tie.

"Good. The girl, too," he ordered.

I didn't understand why he hadn't killed me yet . . . not that I was complaining, but wasn't that the point of the Hastati hunting me down?

"Why?" Simone asked. "She isn't—"

"Do it." He pointed to a handrail by the window. "Tie her to that."

I slid my hands around the metal bar and flinched as Simone pulled the zip-tie around my wrists.

"I'm so sorry, Cassie," Simone repeated.

I nodded, but I couldn't understand how this was happening. None of it made sense. In less than an hour my dad was supposed to wake up and miraculously be able to leave this place. But how was that possible if he was unconscious? Then again, a couple of days ago, I would have considered all of this impossible. I couldn't give up hope.

Footsteps in the hallway pulled me away from my thoughts. Someone was coming in. We might be saved.

The half-eared man hid next to the door, his gun raised and ready.

A woman in a black dress stepped inside, and I immediately recognized the face.

It was Simone's mother. She had called her even though I had specifically told her not to. Now we were either going to be saved or, more likely, there was about to be another hostage. A very valuable hostage.

My heart raced. I had done this to Simone, and now I'd done it to Simone's mother. This was all my fault.

"Mom." Simone's voice had a heavy note of dread in it. I assumed that she was thinking the same thing I was, that her mother was now in danger, too.

Sarah Bimington took one quick look around the room and then turned to face the gunman, sensing his presence by the door.

My breath got caught in my throat. I couldn't imagine things getting any worse.

THIRTY-ONE

"Put that thing away," she ordered, and to my amazement, the half-eared man did so. "I told you to be careful with them, and now the boy is unconscious."

I looked over at Simone for answers, but she was staring at the floor. A sick feeling started to rise up in my chest. *How did Simone's mother know the gunman? Was she Hastati?*

"The boy will be fine," the half-eared man replied. "He attacked and I had to stop him. That is all."

Simone's mother didn't look pleased with the answer, but she turned her attention to Simone, and her face took on a softer appearance. "Sim, honey, where is it?"

Simone hesitated. She looked down and gnawed at one of her fingernails.

My eyes flew back and forth between Simone and her mother, trying to make sense of what was happening.

"Sim, this is for the best." Ms. Bimington's voice dripped with sweetness. "You know that."

"What's going on, Simone?" I couldn't believe what was happening. "Please tell me there's some misunderstanding," I begged. "That your mother isn't Hastati."

She jerked her head up. "No, no. It's nothing like that." She shook her head. "They're not Hastati and no one will hurt you. Not anymore."

"What are you talking about?" I reached out and tried to grab her, forgetting that my hands were tied to the handrail. I pulled against the zip-tie until I felt it cut into my skin.

Simone shuffled her feet and stared at the ground. The only noise in the room came from the beeping monitors.

"Your friend is protecting you, Cassandra," Ms. Bimington answered. "Dante works for me. He explained things to Simone."

"You knew he was working with your mom and you didn't tell us? Simone! Look at me!" I demanded.

Still keeping her eyes down, she tried to explain. "Even if the Hastati have the spear, they'll never let you go. Dante"—she motioned to the half-eared man—"told me my mother's plan and the more I thought about it, the more sense it made."

"And you believe him, a guy who was trying to kill us?" Anger spilled over each word.

"He wasn't going to hurt us. He's not Hastati. We just didn't know that back then." She paused and looked me straight in the eye this time. "Cassie, think about it. Even if they have the spear, the Hastati will want you to use it, or they'll kill you because they'll think someone might get to it through you. They aren't going to let you go back to your old life."

I shook my head in disbelief. "You promised not to tell anyone. I trusted you."

"I told you I'd never put you or your dad in danger, and I won't." She reached out for my hand, but I flicked it away . . .

even with the zip-tie holding me back. "Cassie, this is all to help you. My mother is the only one who can protect you. When she told me this morning that your dad was still in a coma, I knew—"

"This morning! You knew he was like this since this morning and didn't tell me!"

"I . . . I . . . I didn't know how to tell you. You were so sure that he'd be fine, and I knew you'd be angry that I called my mother."

"So you thought this way was better?"

"Cassandra, darling, listen to Simone," Ms. Bimington said with a controlled, patient voice. "When you calm down, you'll see that this is for the best. I will protect you." She took a deep breath. "Now, Simone. We don't have too much time to spare. Go ahead and give me the spear."

I glanced over at Simone's mother. "Why do you want it?" I asked. "Why are you willing to do so much for me?"

"You're Simone's friend, and I want to help." Ms. Bimington smiled, but it wasn't sincere. Her eyes were far too cold. "As for the spear, let's just say I have other plans that don't require your involvement. It's a win-win, my dear."

I stayed quiet. Maybe she didn't know how the spear really worked. And since Simone didn't know I was bound to it, her mother couldn't know, either.

Simone took a few steps toward her mother. "You're sure, right? Nothing will happen to Cassie or her dad. Everything will go back to normal for them."

"Of course I am." She cupped Simone's face with her hand. "Dante will take them to Praiano like you wanted once we've left. Now tell me, where is the spear?"

"Simone, don't," I pleaded. "You can't trust what she's saying."

Simone spun around to face me, her eyes blazing. "She's my mother; of course I trust her!" She strode over to where Asher had dropped his backpack and pulled out my yellow messenger bag. Without a second thought, she yanked out the spear and, tossing the bag aside, gave it to her mother.

"Finally." Ms. Bimington could only stare and marvel at the spear resting in her hands. "I'm so proud of you, Simone." She put the spear in her red leather purse and smiled at me. "You, my dear, are very lucky to have Simone as a friend. I would not offer this kind of protection to just anyone. It will take quite a bit of bargaining and a few concessions on my part. You should be grateful."

I had nothing to say, but venom was spewing from my eyes, aimed straight at Simone.

"Let's just go," Simone whispered to her mother, pulling her arm.

"Fine," she replied. "Go get the elevator. I'll be right there."

Once Simone was out of earshot, Ms. Bimington walked over to where I stood and dropped her voice. "If you make trouble or try to stop me, I will have Dante kill your father, and then he'll kill you." Her eyes narrowed. "I can make it look like an accident. Do you understand me?"

I slowly nodded.

"You are no longer relevant, but Simone seems to care about you, so we're going to let her think I'm protecting you." She stuffed a roll of cash into my pocket. "Truth is, I don't really care what happens to you or your father. So I suggest you use this money to go back to Gregorio and take refuge there." She glanced over at the half-eared man, who had obviously been enjoying the entire scene. "Dante, give her father the serum and meet me downstairs." She walked to the door.

"Wait! What about cutting us free?" I pulled against the zip-ties.

"Ah, yes." Simone's mother smiled. "Cut the boy loose. By the time he wakes up and frees her, we'll be long gone." She spun around on her high heels and walked out of the room.

Dante pulled out a syringe with a long needle.

"What are you doing?" I asked in a panic as he got closer to my father. "What is that?" I pulled against the railing, but the zip-ties wouldn't let me move.

He didn't say a word, but instead tapped the syringe and injected the serum into the IV tube.

"Stop!" I pointlessly ordered. "You're going to kill him."

He pulled out the needle and shook his head. "No. I'm waking him up. Now you be quiet or I'll have her come back." He stepped over Asher and walked to the door.

"No, wait. You're supposed to let him go," I said.

"Am I?" He laughed and walked out of the room.

I stared at my father, but nothing happened. He wasn't miraculously waking up. He wasn't even moving.

"Asher." I stretched, trying to nudge him with my feet, but he was a few inches too far. "Asher!"

I sank to the floor.

This was not how the morning was supposed to end. The spear was gone. Brother Gregorio was dead. My father wasn't waking up.

It felt like I'd lost everything.

—THIRTY-TWO—

Raindrops pelted the window next to me, creating a cadence with the beeps from the machines monitoring my dad's heartbeat. It had been a while since Simone and her mother had left, but I was still afraid of who might show up if I called for help. It was obvious I couldn't trust anyone.

"Ugh," Asher groaned on the floor.

"Asher," I said. "Wake up!"

He squirmed and tried to move his hands, but found that he couldn't.

"What the . . . ?" Asher was now fully awake and rattling the bed as he struggled against the zip-ties. He turned his head and saw that I was tied up, too. "Are you okay?" he asked, a touch of panic in his voice. "Where's Simone? Did that guy take her?"

"No." It hurt to tell him what happened, but I did it. I said exactly how my best friend had betrayed the two of us and given the spear to her mother, who'd been working all along with the half-eared guy.

"I knew not to trust that girl!" Asher exclaimed. "I should've trusted my gut. We have to get you out of here before they realize that you're bound to it!" He grabbed one of his sneakers and pulled off the shoelace.

"Not without my dad." I glanced over at him. He looked so peaceful, like he was sleeping. "I'm not leaving him here."

It was almost noon, but I held out hope that somehow my vision would still be true.

Asher was sitting up and, for some strange reason, he was busily tying a loop on either side of the shoelace. "Fine. But where do we take him? Do you even know if he's in any condition to travel?"

I stayed quiet. I didn't have answers to any of those questions.

Asher draped the shoelace over the zip-tie and put a foot in each loop. He glanced over at me. "Don't worry. We'll figure something out." He started pedaling like he was on a bicycle.

"What are you doing?" I asked.

"Getting free." The zip-tie popped off. "My shoelaces are made of parachute cord. The friction saws the plastic in half." He slid across the floor and slipped the shoelace over my zip-tie. "Here. Now you do it."

I slipped my feet into the loops of the shoelace and pedaled until the zip-tie snapped. Asher was standing next to me, trying to make sense of my father's medical chart.

"According to all of this, your dad suffered some blood loss, but he doesn't look to be too bad. The bullet missed all his organs and he was recovering. He shouldn't be unconscious."

I jumped up and ran to my father's side. Rubbing his hand, trying to get a reaction out of him. "All I know is that I saw him die, and then he was alive again. I don't know why he's unconscious." I glanced at the clock. It was 11:56.

Asher whipped through the pages again. "And there's nothing in here about him dying or being revived."

"Papi, come on." I combed back his hair with my fingers. "We need to get out of here."

"In fact, he was able to communicate this morning. Says he asked to call his daughter."

I stopped what I was doing. "But Simone said her mother told her he was still in a coma this morning. He wasn't responsive."

"Well, we already know that Simone is a liar and can't be trusted. Does it surprise you that she lied about that, too?"

I bit my bottom lip, a part of me still refusing to accept that Simone would betray me completely. "But she really seemed to believe it. Like it was part of the reason she did everything."

"Maybe that's what she wanted you to think." Asher shook his head. "What I still don't get is why her mother only wanted the spear and not you."

I shrugged. "She said she had other plans. I don't think she understands how the spear works. But you should know something else."

"What?" He could tell by the tone in my voice that it was bad.

"When I used the spear, I saw some things in the future . . . besides saving my dad. Really bad things. I didn't tell you before because I thought I could just change it once my dad was safe, but now I don't know."

Asher straightened up and seemed to brace himself for whatever I was about to say. "Tell me."

"It was like a flash-forward with pictures flying by me really fast, and every once in a while a short scene would play out."

"Uh-huh."

"I saw someone being shot, and then there were people in hazmat suits with dead bodies in the street." I could feel the bile rising in my throat. "Are people going to die because of what I've done?"

Asher didn't answer me. He didn't have to. Of course I had done this.

"We're just going to have to figure out a way to get the spear back. Not only to change what you saw, but because Simone's mother will eventually figure things out, and when she does, she'll come after you. No one can resist that much power, so she'll—"

A loud boom shook the whole building as thunder drowned out whatever else Asher said. The clock on the wall showed 11:58. Just like in my vision.

I spun around to look out the window. Outside, through the pelting rain, a white sedan was pulling away. I looked closer and saw Simone sitting in the backseat.

My feelings of despair morphed into anger, then fury. This was all Simone's fault. Because of her we'd lost the spear, and any chance of my fixing things was gone with it. I hated her!

"We need to get out of here. We've been here way too long." Asher poked his head out into the hallway.

I went back to my father and shook him a little by the shoulders. "Papi, please open your eyes. We have to get out of here. Please." I rubbed his arm and then his leg—anything to get his circulation going. "We need you to help us. Figure out where to go."

He didn't react.

It was going to be up to us. We had to find somewhere safe, maybe a remote place out in the countryside. I glanced down at my dad. He was in no condition to go very far. It was going to be hard just getting him to the car. But Asher was right—it would be only a matter of time before someone found us. The monastery wouldn't offer us protection anymore, and we needed an ally. Someone we could trust.

The solution popped into my head. My grandmother! She was connected with powerful people, and the Knights of Malta had never tried to harm me or any of the marked ones. Plus, she'd already offered me protection and saved my life. At least for a day or two, we could find shelter there.

"I know where we can go," I announced. "Back to the Knights of Malta. My grandmother will help . . . I'm sure of it."

Asher made a face. "They really don't like the Hastati."

"Exactly!"

"But I'm—"

"No, your uncle was once Hastati," I said. "You're not."

"I don't know. There are so many unanswered questions. Can we really trust her?"

"Maybe not completely, but it's our best choice. Blood is thicker than water."

"Blood . . ." Asher's eyes widened. "That's what's been bothering me." He opened my dad's hospital chart again.

"Ughhh." A soft moan came from my dad.

I frantically rubbed his arm, then grabbed his hand. "Papi, I'm here. It's me, Cassie." I stroked his forehead, willing him to open his eyes. "Can you hear me? I love you, Papi. To the moon and back."

I felt a slight twitch in his fingers.

"Asher, he's waking up!" The excitement in my voice was unmistakable. This was what mattered. It was worth everything to make sure he was okay. "Whatever they put in his IV is finally working! He's starting to move."

"Um." Asher's demeanor was the exact opposite of mine. "Cassie, I think I may have figured out what happened, but I don't know how to say this."

I peeled my eyes away from my dad's face for a moment to look at Asher. "Just say it."

"Your dad has Type AB blood." Asher pointed to the medical chart.

I rubbed my father's hand, hoping to get some more movement. "So? What does that have to do with anything?"

"Marked descendants have the birthmark in the shape of the spear and Type O blood. You have both of those, right?"

"Yeah. So?" I didn't understand where he was going with all this.

"Someone with Type AB blood can't be the parent of someone with Type O blood. It's basic biology." He paused. "Cassie, this isn't your father."

The beeps from the monitor filled the momentary silence.

What he was saying was ludicrous. "Of course it's him." I glanced down at my father's familiar face. This was the man who had read me bedtime stories, who taught me all about art; he was the only family I'd ever known. "I know what my own father looks like."

"No. I mean he's not your biological father."

"What are you saying? You think I'm adopted?" I threw aside the ridiculous notion. "No, you're wrong. That's crazy. I've seen pictures of my mom pregnant with me and the two of them holding me as a baby. That chart is wrong." I went back to coaxing my dad to wake up. *"Vamos, Papi. Despiértate."*

My dad gave my hand a small squeeze. He could hear me!

"Cassie," Asher continued. "Think about it. It would explain what happened with the spear. The person you connected with and saved was your real father. Your dad, the one in this bed, was never in jeopardy. The chart says he was recovering."

My dad's eyes fluttered open.

"Papi!" I threw my arms around his neck. He was back!

My father slowly reached up for my hands. He gave each one a small kiss. His eyes were watery.

"M'ija," he said in low, hoarse voice. "He's right. I'm not your father."

—THIRTY-THREE—

"Papi, you don't know what you're saying." I took a few steps back, refusing to believe him. "You're still groggy. Asher is wrong."

"No, Cassie." His voice quivered, and he took a deep breath, slowly exhaling. "I love you more than anything, but I should've told you a long time ago. I should've told you everything."

I closed my eyes as my head spun wildly out of control. There was no way it could be true, because if it was, then my entire life was a lie. And if I wasn't Cassie Arroyo, who was I?

I felt dizzy.

"Cassie, are you okay?" Papi asked. "I'm sorry you had to find out like this."

Asher helped me over to a chair.

"It explains a lot, Cassie," Asher said softly. "You have to see that. Your vision makes sense."

I couldn't think about the vision. All I could focus on was that I'd been betrayed and lied to by the one person I thought I could trust completely.

"Vision?" My father lifted his head a little, and the beeps from the heart monitor picked up speed. "What kind of vision?"

Neither Asher nor I said anything.

"Cassie, did you find the spear?" Papi's voice was a little stronger, but there was more fear in it. "Tell me."

"Sir, I think we should get out of here and talk about things later," Asher suggested, glancing out the window.

"And who are you exactly?" Papi's voice had a weird, overly protective tone to it.

"Asher Portaine, Brother Gregorio's nephew. I'm helping Cassie."

"Helping her with what?" My father's eyes narrowed. "What have you two done? Do you have any idea the danger you've put my daughter in by leaving the monastery?"

"We had to," Asher explained. "My uncle died and we came because we thought you—"

"Wait. Gregorio is dead?" Papi ran his fingers through his hair, his brow furrowed liked an accordion. "When?"

"Yesterday," Asher said.

He shook his head. "And you somehow thought bringing her here was a good idea?"

"Seriously?" I shot out of my chair. "You're going to question him? After lying to me my entire life."

"Cassie, *m'ija*." I could see him looking at me like I was still six years old. "I'm your father and I—"

"But you're not! You're not my father!" I spat out the words, wanting them to hurt him as much as saying them out loud hurt me.

"Cassie," he was begging, *"por favor."* He stretched out his arm to reach for me, but I stepped away from him. "I'm trying to protect you. You are and will always be my daughter. Even if we aren't related by blood. There's more to family than biology."

"Yeah," I challenged. "Something like trust and honesty. Maybe that's something I inherited from my *real* father."

The beeping noise from the heart monitor was now driving me crazy. I spun around, grabbed the cord, and yanked it out of the outlet. It felt like I was pulling the plug on everything from my old life.

"*Yo soy tu papá,*" he insisted. "No one loves you more than me." Tears rolled down his cheeks. "I didn't tell you the truth because I wanted to shield you from all this." He leaned over and grabbed my wrist, staring right into my eyes. "I'd give my life for you without hesitation." He took a deep breath. "To the moon and back."

My bottom lip quivered. I'd never seen my father cry. My heart ached.

Papi tugged on my arm, and I didn't resist, collapsing right next to him, careful not to touch his chest where he'd been shot.

There was no way I could stay angry. He was my dad . . . the only one I'd ever known. I just wanted him to hug me and say that everything would be okay. My own tears started to flow as I nuzzled into his neck, and I let all the emotions from the last three days pour out of me.

"I love you, Papi," I whispered as he stroked my hair. "But who am I?"

He gave me a kiss on the forehead, then pushed me back a little to look me right in the eyes. "You are Cassie Arroyo, the same person you've always been."

But he was wrong. I wasn't the same girl from three days ago. Everything had changed. And as much as I wanted him to make it all better, I knew that I was the only one who could fix things.

"Cassie!" Asher, who'd been looking out the window, suddenly spun around. "We need to get out of here right now!" He darted to the door and looked down the hallway. "The motorcycle guy from Civita just walked into the building."

"The who?" Papi asked.

"The Hastati who shot you," I said, trying to get my dad to sit up. "Can you walk?"

He slapped the side of his thighs as he struggled to move from the bed. "Cassie, I can't feel my legs!"

"What?" I threw off the blanket and shook his bare legs.

Asher pulled me away from him. "We have to leave!"

"No!" I jerked my arm away. "I'm not leaving without my father. We didn't do all of this not to have him come with us!"

"I can't do it," Papi said softly, a resigned look on his face. "I'd only hold you back. Plus, they aren't after me, they're coming for you."

It all came down to choices.

Both the gypsy in the subway station and Signora Pescatori had told me the same thing . . . *choices determine destiny*. It was time I made my choice and embraced my destiny.

"Okay, listen, Papi. You have to make your way to the Knights of Malta compound. Dame Elisabeth, Mom's mother . . . my grandmother, is there. We can trust her."

My father's eyes grew wider. "How did . . . ?" He shook his head. "Never mind. Dame Elisabeth at the Knights of Malta. Got it."

I bent down and gave him a kiss on the cheek. "To the moon and back."

"Cassie!" Asher was holding the door open. "We don't have time!"

"Go!" Papi said.

No longer hesitating, I followed Asher down the stairs to the ground floor. Pushing open the door, I noticed that the rain had completely stopped, but the dark clouds remained.

"Gisak is over there." Asher pointed to the old car parked across the lot. He scanned the area, checking to see if it was all clear.

"Asher," I said, realizing that my choices now affected him, too. "You need to know that I'm done running."

"What?" He glanced from me to the car, then back to me. "We have to race over. We don't know who might be watching."

"No, I mean I'm not going to run away. I won't live looking over my shoulder all the time. I'm going to go after them and get the spear."

"Can we talk about this later?" Desperation filled his voice. "First we need to get out of here."

"Fine," I said, but I knew things were going to be different.

I was done being a target.

It was time I returned fire.

—ACKNOWLEDGMENTS—

Being a writer is such an adventure. From the quiet excitement of discovering an idea that has been lurking in your imagination to the joyful anxiety of having your book shared with the world—it can be quite the thrill ride. But a writer doesn't do it alone. This story would never have seen the light of day had it not been for the involvement, support, and encouragement of a legion of friends, family, and talented professionals. It is thanks to them that this book exists.

Beginning with my wonderful agent, Jen Rofé, who believed in this crazy story of mine from the very beginning. Thank you for pushing me forward even when I doubted myself. I'm so glad you're on my team!

As always, my amazing family has my back during the entire writing process. My husband and sons cheered me on—even when that meant listening to my mutterings about urban legends and ancient artifacts during dinner or in the middle of a soccer game. My parents, sister, brother-in-law, mother-in-law, aunts, uncles, and cousins continued to show their love and support by being my "backup" when real life interfered with my writing time. I love you all!

Then there are my incredibly talented writing friends: Danielle Joseph, Gaby Triana, Alexandra Alessandri, Stephanie Hairston, Alexandra Flinn, Adrienne Sylver, Marcea Ustler, Linda Rodriguez Bernfeld, and Lorin Oberweger. These lovely ladies gave me critical feedback and advice. Some of them even heard fifteen variations of the same chapter and still didn't smack me upside the head! *Grazie mille!*

To Ed Masessa, your sound advice helped me immensely and your enthusiasm for this book is contagious. May you live long and prosper, my Trekkie friend.

Thank you is not enough for my two fantastic editors, Emily Seife and David Levithan, who helped shape this story into everything I hoped it could be. Another big box of Cuban *pastelitos* doesn't come close to expressing my appreciation, but I'll send them anyway.

Iacopo Bruno and Phil Falco, who created the best cover I could have imagined, thank you for honoring my words with your beautiful illustration and design. It's perfect!

Finally, but always first in my life, I thank God for all my many blessings, including this dream job where I get to share stories and connect with my readers. I am truly grateful.

—ABOUT THE AUTHOR—

CHRISTINA DIAZ GONZALEZ is the award-winning author of *Return Fire*, the sequel to *Moving Target*, as well as *The Red Umbrella*, which was named an ALA Best Book for Young Adults and called an "exceptional historical novel" by *Kirkus Reviews*, and *A Thunderous Whisper*, which was heralded by the Children's Book Council as a Notable Social Studies Book. She lives in Florida with her husband and two sons. Learn more at www.christinagonzalez.com.

CASSIE'S ADVENTURES CONTINUE!

CHRISTINA DIAZ GONZALEZ

RETURN FIRE

THE SEQUEL TO MOVING TARGET